FOR EVERY EVIL UNDER THE SUN

ALEXANDRA BURT   V.P CHANDLER   LAURA OLES

Foreword by
SCOTT MONTGOMERY

FREDONIA INK
PUBLISHING

 Formatted with Vellum

For every evil under the sun,
There is a remedy, or there is none.
If there be one,
try and find it;
If there be none,
never mind it."

— Mother Goose Rhyme

CONTENTS

FOREWORD

It's not every day that I am asked to write the foreword for a collection of crime fiction written by female authors. I'm mainly connected with fiction that leans on the high testosterone side; if it has a tough guy, a gun, and a dangerous dame, you've met me halfway.

As someone with a long career in this space, I know that women in this genre have long informed, shaped, and contributed to the ongoing evolution of crime stories, providing both entertainment and social commentary. I consider myself both a fan and a champion of their influence.

If you are looking for the best in crime fiction, the women in the genre have always stood out. Margaret Millar, Dorothy B. Hughes, Helen Nielsen, and others looked at the shadowy undercurrents of post-World War Two life and were as popular as their contemporaries if not reprinted as much after. Many of them went into places even Mickey Spillane's Mike Hammer feared to tread. Today, the likes of Megan Abbott, Laura Lippman, and Attica Locke have taken the genre into new and exciting directions. And now we have Alexandra Burt, V.P. Chandler, and Laura Oles.

What you are about to read are three writers taking the dark torch and running with it. They have no problem bringing the bad.

Like filmmakers Billy Wilder and Robert Siodomak, **Alexandra Burt** continues the tradition of European immigrants looking at America with a noir eye. Her psychological thrillers explore the bleakest parts of human behavior and produce some of the most violent and unnerving stories without a bullet fired or knife slashed. Her writing can be so disturbing you might not notice the dry wit she peppers it with.

V.P. Chandler stakes her claim in a genre practically her own —frontier noir. She writes in a time and place where society and law may have gotten to the cities and towns, but out in the prairie and plains you still have to make your own justice. Her west is brutal and her heroines prove capable of meeting it head-on.

Laura Oles is a student of crime fiction. With her firm sense of setting and a storytelling pitch others would kill for, she explores the dynamics of seriously dysfunctional families. Her sibling and parental relationships show the conditions of unconditional love.

Here are three authors with stories of characters at their most questionable. Many of them have the brightest of locations, whether under a California or Texas sun or Vegas and Tokyo lights. That said, these writers aren't afraid of the dark. They thrive in it.

Scott Montgomery, 2024
Editor of "Austin Noir"

PART I

THERE IS A REMEDY, OR THERE IS NONE

L isten.

The sun watches from her rightful place in the sky. She is ever-present. Life-giving, yes—but also relentless. All my life, the weary and scorched forms she creates have haunted me. She shines on the strange and broken, but also on the strong and resilient. She thickens skin. She strains at the leash. She contains multitudes.

Her rays are stirring up something, always readjusting themselves. She warms rabbits in their cages; cascades honeyed light on a surfer clinging to her board; keeps an eye on an old farmhouse rattling in the wind. What does she know that you don't? Time is meaningless. Places are arbitrary. Her loss cannot be reversed. Whatever deed is done is done.

She is a seed. A seed that makes the world grow. Listen as she speaks. Prepare yourself.

Something is about to happen.

Alexandra Burt

ECHO BEACH, 1982

BY ALEXANDRA BURT

Previously published in *Mystery Tribune*

The day is perfect. The sun has nestled herself in the sky, her rays are bleeding into the ocean below. I wrap my arms around my legs, feeling the warmth of the sand seeping through the towel, while the breeze dries my hair. Salty brine hangs in the air, the waves are lacy, and sea foam inches its way toward me just to retreat.

There is a man, up by the low wooden fence, where the sand meets concrete. He sits motionless. His hands are deep in the pockets of his shorts. We are on the far side of the beach, by the wedge, at the southeast end of the peninsula. Bluffs to our right, cliffs to our left, the hillside with dotted lights behind us like lightning bugs trapped in a jar shaped like a mesa. The man is watching me.

It's just me and him now on the deserted stretch of beach. I have seen this man before. He watched me with a smile on his face earlier as I centered myself on the board, back arched, paddling out into the surf. I ignored him then. I do not smile at men in general, and maybe that is my downfall.

~

The day at Echo Beach starts early in the morning, long before the sun comes up. Under the guise of applying for jobs, I borrow my mother's car. I drop her off at Hoag Hospital, where she works the day shift as a nurse. I smile as she mouths *good luck* and I wave as I pull off. Back home, I slide my surfboard onto the back seat of my mother's crème Chrysler Fifth Avenue. I fight my way into my wet suit. In a bag, I stuff a beach towel and a tube of Zinka.

I graduated from high school the year before. My mother threw me a *Class of 1981* party but within weeks all my friends scattered to colleges or jobs and the days unfold anticlimactically. My mother drops college names and career choices, but I just want to be on the beach. Every job or chore is nothing but a distraction from surfing. Surfing is everything. My body vibrates with anticipation as soon as I pull up at a beach. The sand beneath me burns the bottom of my feet as if to say *hurry, do not miss out.* When the surf billows and swells, I drop my Red Rails board, a graduation gift from my mother, into the ocean. The center of the board has a rich, deep stained strip from bottom to top, lined with black pinstripes as if in mourning. I paddle, my eye on the horizon, waiting for a wave, *the* wave, that catapults me into a state of buoyancy. I paddle and paddle and paddle. I never tire. I never want to stop.

That day, I cross Balboa Bridge and drive all the way to the Island instead of my regular spot by the Bay Resort. Why? Maybe because my mother's questions have turned pesky with each passing day, maybe I caught traffic lights at the perfect moment shaving a quarter of an hour from my route, or maybe there was no reason at all. If there was, I forget.

When I get to Echo Beach, the sun rises from the ocean and the magic unfolds as I watch a fiery orb tinting the ocean vermilion. I listen to the wind whispering in my ears as it plays with my hair. I wonder later, much later, when everything unfolds, if the wind was trying to tell me something and I failed to listen.

The man is still there. He walks in my direction; the water's edge is a map for him to get to me as the waxing and waning sea foam leads him to my spot in the sand. His gait is long and awkward, as if he suffers from some sort of old injury, not allowing him to bend his knees. Stiff. Unlike his hair, shaggy and unkempt, whipping about his shallow face. His skin is tanned as if he spends a lot of time in the sun. He is so close to me I can see the blond hairs on his legs.

I recall an article I read a while back, one I at first would not read at all—about some offhand danger like escaping from a sinking car, something no one thinks will ever happen to them —but I skimmed it after all. It was about not being a victim. My thoughts tumble like Jenga blocks. *If you have a bad feeling, do not think you are paranoid. Predators target those they consider the weakest and most vulnerable.*

The man is now standing with his feet in the ocean and as the tide covers him up to his ankles; he bends over and digs in the sand with his fingers. That is when I make my move. I stuff the towel in my bag and grab my surfboard. I carry the board forward so the fins point away from me, the bottom of the board resting against my body, like a shield. I turn to see if he is still where I saw him last, by the shoreline. He is gone. No, there he is. He has moved back to the low wooden fence, close to the spot where he sat earlier, but now he stands by the gap, the gap I need to pass through to get to the car. He is blocking the gap. He is waiting for me.

Do not be distracted by anything. Never walk with your head down and do not keep your hands in your pockets, do not.

In my mind, I attempt to assemble more bits and pieces of the article but there is only the breathless beating of my heart in my chest. Maybe I should speak to him to show him he has picked the wrong victim.

Do not appear frightened, confused, or distracted.

The board's leg rope drags in the sand, and I panic. What should I have done? Taken it off and stuffed it in my bag? Wrap it around my wrist? The article said nothing about ropes. I am giving him a weapon; I am literally aiding him in my demise.

I focus. It is too late to avoid him now. I am five feet away from him, which is less than the length of my body. It does not seem far enough; he is tall, so much taller than I thought. He towers over me.

Show him you will not be the perfect victim. Present yourself with confidence.

He says something I cannot make out. His voice is honeyed, not to be trusted, almost seductive, but not in a good way.

"What?" I ask, and my chest heaves under the pressure. Even this one word sounds breathless when I try so hard to appear fearless.

"Something's wrong with your car," his voice sounds matter-of-factly as he repeats it.

Be aware of the message your body sends. If I stand tall, remain calm, and respond confidently and assertively, I will be fine.

Keep your wits about yourself.

I want to run, but how far would I get? I want to scream, but who would hear me? I want to not be here; I want to be home, want to wait for my mother, watch her as she enters through the back door at the end of the day, in her hand a bag with a large grease spot on the bottom, the scent of burgers or hot dogs or tacos slowly wafting toward me.

Your wits, keep them.

The man beholds me. He is calm, not as if he is about to grab me and drag me behind the cliffs nearby. No, he is calm as if he is studying me, as if he is assessing the situation. He is wondering if he can make his move now. He is determined to do something that he usually keeps locked away in the crawlspaces of his mind. Until he finds a victim. And I am the victim. He is about to kill me, but instead of grabbing me, he is smiling at me with his lips pulled upward. But his eyes, his eyes are empty.

"My car?" I ask. "What about it?"

"Well," he says, "someone did a number on it while you were surfing."

I pivot left and right because he is blocking my view. I see the hood of my mother's Chrysler propped open. I know nothing about cars. Nor about danger, about not being a victim, except that one article I read; how can I possibly escape a man like him? A man who lingers until dark. A man so tall. Looming. With hands so big. How peculiar he is. Like an island. I cannot imagine him in his life, his natural surroundings. I cannot, for the life of me, figure out if he is married or young enough to live with his parents, or maybe he lives in his aunt's basement. He looks unkempt with his scraggly hair and tanned skin, not leathery but getting there, rather dull up close. I see white lines on his arms, as if something has taken off a layer of skin, exposing the dermis underneath. Scabbed over, but now healed. Something he tries to hide, but can't.

"You saw someone messing with my car?" I ask, my voice taut.

"I didn't know whose car it was. I thought they were fixing it or something. I waited until everybody left." He puts his hands back in his pockets.

"Okay," is all I say.

"I think they just pulled off a hose or a gasket or something. I can help you get it running."

A plan. I need a plan.

"I have tools. I can fix it," he points behind him. A van sits in the dark, backed in, pointing toward the street. As if prompted, the parking lot lights come on, illuminating his face. He is now bathed in a yellow hue.

I want to breathe a sigh of relief. I want to believe that this is what this is; a kind stranger helping, and I realize dangers are a peculiar thing. They are everywhere and nowhere all at once.

I turn toward him. I even smile.

"Let me see if the car starts."

I have a plan. I will get in the car and lock the doors. I will blow my horn to alert people. There are people around, maybe not right here, but there must be people close by. We cannot possibly be all alone here. We cannot.

"I doubt it," he says.

"You doubt what?"

"That it starts. But try."

It is then that I feel his hand on my shoulder. His fingers sear into my flesh, his palm vibrates on my naked skin. As quickly as he touches me, he just as quickly thinks otherwise. Or maybe he was just confused and pulled back his hand? He slides my surfboard from my hands, opens the back door, and tucks it onto the back seat.

"Let me give you a hand with this," he says, and closes the door with a thud that makes me cringe. The thud sounds like a blunt object impacting a skull. I do not know how my mind comes up with this. Maybe my perception is enhanced by my impending death?

I climb in the front seat and dig for my keys in my bag, insert it into the ignition. I turn the key and I pray *please please please.*

Not a sound. I twist the key again. Nothing.

His disembodied voice reaches me from behind the propped-up hood, his words monotonous and low. "Hold on," he says, "I think I know what the problem is."

I only see his crotch in the gap between the hood and the dashboard. As he bends down to inspect something about the engine, his face comes into focus.

"Try again," he calls out.

I turn the key and reluctantly the motor purrs to life. The hood slams shut. I look for him through the windshield, but he is no longer standing in the reddish-orange cast of the street-light. I whip my head around. He opens the driver's door, his large hands reaching for me. He is making his move; I just know it. I freeze, wait for some sort of impact or knife or whatever else he has in store for me. But he just turns the control arm attached to the base of the steering wheel. "Don't forget to turn on the lights," he says. "It's dark."

I want to open my mouth to scream, but I step on the gas. I speed off and as the Chrysler tilts, centrifugal forces slam the door shut. In my ears echoes the sound of my heart, like a train speeding over tracks.

What am I supposed to tell my mother about that night? Maybe I should spare her the details and just tell her I went to the beach, and that I lied when I told her I would look for a job and that I have learned my lesson? Or do I tell her a stranger approached me by the beach and he had hands so large that just one could have strangled me? Maybe I should go to the police and tell an officer, blow by blow, how the day unfolded? But what would that look like? That I had lied to my mother and spent the day at the beach surfing, how I forgot the time and suddenly the sun was about to go down and a stranger came to help me get my car running? How do I explain that as the man told me, he would help me fix the car, there was a certain pitch in the caws of the seagulls, a lazy hesitation in the way the wind picked up just to go quiet?

That night is like pieces of film on the cutting room floor; I do not know what to do with the individual fragments. I go over the details in my mind, over and over, asking myself if I got away from a killer or if I spit gravel in the face of a good Samaritan? Which one is it?

This plays out in my mind for days and I go back and forth; one day the man is a helpful stranger, the next a killer of women under the cover of darkness. But I am only kidding myself. That is what it comes down to. After days of reflection, I conclude: I have an instinct for volatility. All that hairpulling at playgrounds, all that body-blocking in high school, those gatekeepers telling me to do as they say. How tables have turned at the drop of a dime, from play to out of hand before I even have time to take a breath.

A mark has been put on me when his hand touched my shoulder. I have contracted a virus that has invaded my bloodstream. It is circulating, mutating any which way. The pressure, how I still feel the pressure on my skin, fear comes and goes like aftershocks of an earthquake, they rattle me. Safety is on the other side of those feelings, but I just cannot get there.

Weeks later, I find my mother in the living room, glued to the TV. We sit in silence as we watch the news anchor relay the details. He is all square jaw and deep voice, hair neatly parted, and I take only a minute or two to process what he is saying. Echo Beach. A man killed a girl. She was seventeen. Beaten. Raped. Strangled. Left by the cliffs, a stone's throw from where I sat that day. A girl just like me. But with the rope. A rope that has a loop in which you slip your foot, which attaches to the surfboard to stop it from floating away after you fall off. A rope, thick and sturdy, almost seven feet long. Still wrapped around her neck when they found her.

When his mugshot appears in the upper left corner of the screen, all life drains from me and I cry. My mother hugs me, strokes my hair, like she did when I was a little girl.

"I got away," I say with a shaky voice.

That is the moment my mother's face turns gray. Her hands are interlaced and fidgety as I go on. I am nervous and wordy, but she holds my gaze. She never interrupts me, nor does she take her eyes off me. And I tell her how I saw the man, how I forgot the time and before I knew it the sun was setting and the hood was propped up, and his large hands offered help and tools and he touched my shoulder.

He killed the girl days after I encountered him on Echo Beach. I wonder why he spared me, but not her. He could have dragged me off into the darkness but he created a narrative with the car and the propped-up hood. But that was just an interlude. A game he played with me, a buildup for something else: I was the foreplay for the actual act.

Nothing is the same after that day. Not the waves, not the sand, not the sun rising nor setting. I move to Las Vegas a month later, which is not a plan. As such, it just seems like a necessary thing to do. I don't want to be reminded of that summer. I want to get away where there are no beaches and no ocean and no surfing. The surfboard I left behind collects dust in my mother's garage. I plan on taking classes at UNLV but for now I work as a show-girl. I wear a costume, a leotard, and giant red and silver feather wings strapped onto my back, and I take photos with tourists. Walking the streets at night through crowds, I feel safe. Anything but an abandoned beach and a setting sun. Sometimes, as we showgirls scoot together to fit into the frame of a camera, a hand will brush against my shoulder and touch the very spot he had touched. I go home on those nights and my heart races all night and in the early morning hours I watch a tiny sliver of sunlight creep between buildings.

"I got away," I whisper to myself. Over and over.

I focus on the mountain range in the far distance. When the sun turns into a ball, almost too bright to look at, I stare straight into it, and I want to peel my skin off.

LACY'S WINGS AS CLEAR AS GLASS
BY ALEXANDRA BURT

Lacy stared at the phone display, then tucked it in her back jeans pocket. She had been waiting for the call for weeks. She had auditioned for a role in a science fiction movie to play one of many angelic creatures—the one with the most lines. That's the role she wanted, not one creature idly standing by; no, she wanted a part of the action. Lines, impact, her face in closeup. That's how you make a name for yourself, after all.

"Think Joe Black and City of Angles," the woman had said, handing her the lines to read on a single piece of paper.

Joe Black. She found herself unable to think of anything else since. Joe Black. One of her favorites, no, the favorite. Death personified is a role of a lifetime, Lacy thought. If only she were given a chance.

As she read the lines, her heart pounded with excitement and anxiety in that dimly lit casting room. She wasn't naïve. Everything in this town was about knowing people or knowing people who know people, and Lacy knew no one. In the bustling heart of Hollywood, she was but another talented, struggling actor waiting for her big break.

The phone wasn't going to ring. These calls come at a

specific time. She had overheard the comment when she worked as a barista at a trendy coffee shop on Sunset Boulevard, where she had mastered the delicate skill of frothing milk and serving celebrities on their way to auditions and red-carpet events. While pouring lattes and crafting cappuccinos, she overheard the latest industry buzz and gleaned insights into upcoming productions.

Nobody hires before ten or after four," said a thirty-something who couldn't be bothered to put down the phone as Lacy prepared his order. The line stretched back to the door, but Lacy remained calm. The guy wore some band t-shirt below a distressed leather jacket and a chunky ring on his right hand. She had seen him before; the guy seemed to live in his yellow-tinted sunglasses.

"Why don't we just look for some more people," tinted glasses said, pointing at the venti size and mouthing "Americano." "Can't be hard to find someone," he said before quickly hanging up. He swiped his phone over the contactless reader. A checkmark appeared on the display, and yellow glasses was gone.

Lacy hadn't gathered enough info who the guy was or what studio he worked for, but someone at the back of the line called out to him, "What's up, Roger Ward? Long time no see."

And that's how Lacy found out about the audition for the movie.

But the call never came. All those workshops she had attended, all those networking events, all those jobs as extras in films and TV shows. She had taken even the smallest role as an opportunity to showcase her talent, even if it meant playing a nameless face in the background. She had waited for weeks and then she thought about what she had kept at bay all those years: there would not be a movie, there would not be a breakout role. This might just be the end of the road.

She cringed at her own naivete. She was far removed from the girl she had been when she had arrived in Los Angeles with stars in her eyes, armed with a head full of dreams and a resume full of small theater roles. She'd moved to LA when she was in her late twenties, and now she was pushing thirty with nothing to show. Did she turn heads? Yes, she did, but clueless she was not. Tastes change and directors were ever so critical; a boob job might open one door but close another. She was critical of her looks but saw no need to change herself—and anyway; she was dammed if she did, damned if she didn't.

She had imagined a much different life. She had envisioned catching film shoots in progress from her very window. A few car chase scenes or a character scene in a tiendita two buildings down the street. Not once in all those years had Lacy seen cop cars blocking the road or helicopters flying above. To anybody, this would be rather boring—how they filmed the same two-second scene over and over and over—but to Lacy, even the theory of such things was sheer adrenaline. Everything about movies was magical to her; the trailers the stars use and the cables everywhere. This was her world. Nothing else would do. But the streets were snaking strangely in a maze she had never navigated. Those palm trees everywhere seemed cartoonish now. She had never frequented the trendy brunch spots or the rooftop bars, instead, she had ended up in endless menial jobs. And just when she thought she would not make rent, another job came along.

This time it was a night shift security job at a studio. At first, the frigid, air-conditioned room with the ergonomic office chair in front of two dozen monitors seemed tedious but then Lacy caught some sort of technical bug and every day she looked forward to the monitors neatly quartered into four equal squares, displaying four different angles of the same room. There were no less than 300 Lorex security cameras tucked into corners and stuck onto the ceilings. Each one had rounded, multi-faceted eyes protruding from their elongated plastic bodies.

All those alarm panels and call boxes, intrusion monitoring devices and video motion detection systems, all those security alarms, Lacy felt she had gone from a clueless worker bee to a prolific observer of the film world. And so she watched the comings and goings of actors and directors until the studio lights went out. And still she sat, staring at those monitors. A thought popped into her mind: this is as close as I'll ever come to being on a set. She concentrated on the cameras as they hummed up and down, sideways, backwards, and forward. With the push of a button, she was in control of millions of lenses, their movement subject to her every command. Nothing would pass by her; nothing would go undetected—nothing.

Of course, there were drawbacks besides working nights. She had developed headaches and blurry vision from staring at the screens for hours. She saw this as a step closer to getting a role. One that would showcase her true talents. Just show up, Lacy reminded herself, and maybe, just maybe, some director would pause at her desk and look at her over the numerous screens and say "Hey, I think you'd be perfect for a role I have in mind," and she'd say, "I'm an actress, we're both in luck," and then her life would change. She just knew it. Grit was half the rent, being prepared the other.

One early morning in June, before the sun had risen, Lacy had a seizure during her shift. She knew what it was the moment it happened—she'd seen enough movies to know. She lay there, urine-soaked, swallowing her tongue, neck snapping, legs kicking, eyes rolling in the back of her head. Eventually the day shift showed up, called an ambulance, and two burly guys with orange vests strapped her to a gurney. She refused a ride to the hospital—that bill would be outrageous and she was all but broke.

The very next day, her boss, Larry Donahue, called her into his office. Lacy knew what was coming. Donahue wore his Safe-Corp uniform badly and his name, 'Larry,' was stitched on his chest in cursive, almost illegible in all capital letters. A more complicated name would have been hard to decipher. Lacy's name was borderline legible, but the dayshift had a guy named Carrington and he caught hell more than once. They called him everything from Constantine to Capricorn.

Larry opened the manila folder in front of him, shifted some papers from one side to the other, and strained to read with his enormous glasses infested with fingerprints. Lacy wondered if Larry allowed his kids to play with them. The meeting was brief —all Lacy would remember later was something about "new opportunities," and "it's not for everyone," and the envelope slid across the desk. Her last paycheck.

On her way home, she stopped by a liquor store. A headache had developed behind her right eye. By the time Lacy arrived, got to the 15th floor of her apartment building with a bottle of Johnny Walker in hand, her head was being squeezed so tight she thought it was going to pop. She loved the building. It was old, far from the construction of modern condos with well-worn hardwood floors and vintage tiling, and other quirky features.

The windows were drafty, and she often wondered what held the building in place.

She'd have to move—she wouldn't be able to afford this place much longer. An almost physical pang, somehow both dull and sharp, accompanied that realization, as if a knife was being twisted in her gut. From the couch, a tumbler of Johnny Walker in hand, she admired the views of the Hollywood streets.

Her senses dulled after the third tumbler. She longed to add ice but couldn't get herself to move. Unemployment wouldn't hold her over for long. She thought of applying at the liquor store where she had bought the bottle, where a flyer on the sliding glass door read "HIRING." She would have to stock shelves, chase homeless people away from the parking lot, sweep the floors. The manager, a middle-aged man named Jody with horrendous teeth and arms covered in liver spots, would be her boss.

As she stared at the tawny whiskey bottle, she imagined getting hit on while packing brown paper bags for the men who handed out street flyers on the nearby corner. She—a cashier in a liquor store? Lacy cringed. She was five-nine and athletic, not the average actress. Her front teeth overlapped slightly, but she was pretty in a generic sense, and all she needed was to be seen by somebody in the industry. One stroke of luck, one sleight of hand, one moment of the fates smiling at her.

She poured two finger's worth into the whiskey tumbler and raised it. The whiskey seemed to glow as if she were looking through a lens, no, as if she were staring into the sun. Rich gold liquid with amber glints. She gently placed the rim of the glass on her upper lip just beneath her nose. Notes of soft raisins, toffee, fresh malt, and light cream. The first sip tasted of a hint of oak, specs of almonds and marzipan and at the end, there was a finish of honeyed spices. The drink went down, burning her stomach. The bottle was a gold label edition, the last one she could afford for a while. Lacy pulled the bottle closure deliberately, circling around exactly three times, starting at the lip, ending at the collar. It was a scene from a James Bond movie she had seen decades ago, and even then, she had dreamed about being a female Bond character. How perfect she'd be for it. She'd do all the stunts herself.

The phone rang, piercing the air. Lacy flinched but didn't spill her drink. She let it ring. The pounding behind her eyes had become unbearable and her eyeballs felt as if they were being pushed out of their sockets. She heard a distinct humming sound, like a tiny insect flapping its wings close to her ears.

She got up from the couch and changed into her running gear. She was an avid runner, and a sweat-breaking, lungs-huffing jog usually cured all ills. Nothing to do but run off this headache.

Before she even put one foot in front of the other, she must have run miles: how else could she explain those breathtaking views? She had never seen this mountain before, so close to the city. This was not the street she lived on but how to explain she hadn't even hiked up a hill yet, but there she stood at the foot of a steep incline, the valley stretched out below her. Was it the whiskey? Or the seizure? Yes, the seizure most likely—ever since the seizure, her brain had a mind of its own. She couldn't explain it any other way. She had no control, could be at one place one moment, an entirely different place the next. In fact, she couldn't remember how she got home after she had grabbed her last paycheck.

Then a thought manifested, powerful and lasting: she was Catwoman! How timid she had been in her movements before, when she was really a powerful feline trapped in an already athletic body. Where she had slouched before, she was now light on her feet. Why did her arm feel so heavy? That must be the whip—yes, she'd make an expert hunter. She could fix her gaze on prey, slinky and free as she moved about. She was Michelle Pfeiffer, discovering her feminine power! She was—was—was losing her mind—she felt as if—

Lacy awoke on the couch with the TV running. What time it was, she wasn't sure. How long she'd been asleep, she didn't know. It wasn't dark yet, but how could it not be? Surely hours must have passed.

She sat up, her head pounding even louder than before. On her way to the bathroom, the hallway seemed long and confusing. Her hands were sweaty, and her heart was beating out of her chest. She looked in the bathroom mirror and didn't recognize herself. She had featured in a print ad for perfume five years back or so, where she stood in front of a large window overlooking a city lighting up the night with a blanket of glitter below. In that ad she wore a baby-blue satin dress, Manolo heels, and her hair was as glossy as a doll's. She had always thought she'd looked dainty in that ad, with hands like a nine-year-old. She had exuded superiority.

Now she stared at herself in the mirror. Lacy had an odd feeling suddenly; a sneaking suspicion her body was up to something she was not prepared for. Everything expanded in front of her eyes; she no longer saw the bathroom in its entirety —the walls had moved inward. Shifted. The pressure behind her eyes became unbearable with every second that ticked by. She tried to focus on her hands. They were no longer the small hands from the ad, no longer shaking, but to her surprise, the sleeves of her running shirt were at least two inches too short. Her wrists were visible; the veins like blue, powerful rivers running through her. She did not remember the sleeves being so short when she had put the shirt on earlier.

That pressure behind her eyes was like a steamroller, and her back was tingling as if she had carried a backpack for too long. She could not speak; her mouth was dry. She couldn't part her lips. Her shoulder blades were on fire, and she couldn't stand them being touched by the fabric any longer. She pulled off her shirt.

Should she call an ambulance? Where was her phone? She stood in the hallway, trying to get her bearings, and used her shirt to wipe her forehead. She was drenched in sweat. Her whole body was in a state of growth. Her eyes were popping out of her head; it was no longer just a feeling—no, they were coming out of the sockets as if something were pushing on them from inside her head. Her sleeves, God help her, were even shorter than they had been a few minutes ago. They reached barely past her elbows.

As she passed by the large window and looked outside, she instantly felt a sense of calm. The height tranquilized her, soothed her. She rested her forehead against the cold glass. Her eyes looked gigantic in the windowpane.

She couldn't think straight. Her thoughts jumbled. How long do seizures last? Not knowing what to do, she poured herself another whiskey. She dozed off—at least, that's what she thought.

The next time she had a clear thought, it wasn't a thought at all. She was incapable of thinking, but she was present within herself. Her body soared upwards. Wait, where was she? A dream—surely this was a dream. There was that mountain again, that cosmic mountain. Snowcapped. There were stars. And clouds. Why were the stars in a half circle? What constellation was this? She was deeply aware of her body, the flapping of her clothes and the soft hum in her ears. She never wanted the moment to end. She was up in the air somehow, wasn't she? Her relationship with air was so intimate that she did not understand how she could have lived without this intimacy until then.

There was no time. No day, no night. She developed a sudden aversion to Johnny Walker. The smell sickened her. The disgust developed over time, though she was not aware of how much time, or how little. Or if there even was time. She just knew she hated the smell of it. She sat on the couch flying again over that same mountain, past those same stars. The same clouds.

But there was more.

First, she fought the desire. A desire she was so baffled by that all she could do was give in to it: she felt the urge to eat the flies that had ventured into her apartment. She squashed them against the windowpane, then licked them off. She thought of a hairy feline tongue, but no, this was different. She had nothing to compare it to, but it felt as if her upper lip had taken over her face and the lower mouthpart shot out to capture pea-green bowels and brains that reminded her of miniature road kill. Her tongue left a trail of mucus behind. The window was covered in silvery tracks of a gluelike substance, with more and more flies trapped within it. Her eyesight was off—way off. Everything seemed larger than she remembered it. Most colors had completely disappeared. Whatever it was, it had gotten the better of her.

The pain in her back had progressed then, she felt immeasurable agony as she tried to stand tall to reach the window and the bugs. Her body was now elongated, her pants were baggy around the hips and ended below her knees. Time passed, or rather must have passed, and her only nourishment were the flies swarming the leftovers on the counter. She felt her body getting out of hand. She couldn't find the words, but there was a clear realization: her almost weightless body was having a life of its own. And she did not know how to stop it.

Lacy explained all of it to herself. She had to. After all, this couldn't be random—there had to be an explanation. And so she came up with a story. Her eyes, so round, so large, so dark: they were turning into bug eyes. She was, damn her if it wasn't true, she was The Fly. He was Seth Brundle saying, I'm an insect who dreamt he was a man and loved it. But now the dream was over... and the insect was awake. She realized the seizure had changed her, given her the power to become something else entirely. Her body growing—that was her way of becoming, well, some sort of creature. A moth? Something larger, even? Something that could soar and stand on top of the same mountain. A dragonfly? There were the same stars. The same clouds. And somehow, she hadn't moved at all.

In the dead of night, with all color gone and her world merely shades of gray, she thought about ramming her body into the window. She threw herself into the pane, once, twice, three times. Then she stopped counting until she heard the glass shatter. She climbed through the shards and then she stood on a ledge. Only meant to give the visual illusion of a balcony, the wrought-iron railing had been long removed. Lacy stood on the ledge and allowed the wind to gently sway her body. She took a deep breath, spread her arms. A realization then—too late. Her mind put it together then. She knew death when she saw it: like in Catwoman, one can only be fooled for so long. She had not died, but somehow come back to life even more powerful.

Then the pieces clicked into place: click, click, click.

Paramount. The snowcapped peaks. The clouds. The drums. The ferocious roar of the Metro Goldwyn Mayer lion.

Her body had already taken a step, and before she knew it, she was treading air. This realization didn't change a thing for her. She enjoyed the humming sensation vibrating through her body. She wouldn't change it for anything. Where her arms used to be, she realized a new growth. They were not arms, not the elongated limbs she recalled that had shed her clothes—no, they were, they were—she could hardly believe it: giant, lacy wings, as clear as glass. Soon it would become day and the sun would rise and stretch out her golden arms. Lacy willed her wings to move and to her surprise they propelled her upwards, downwards, backwards, forwards, side to side, and she even hovered in midair! So strong yet so flexible. Not even the strongest headwind would slow her down. But it wasn't day yet. It was night, still. And so she soared, taking in the dark night, the twinkling lights of Los Angeles unmistakably in the distance. Among those lights, somewhere within the sea of them, there was a film studio.

If only they could see her now. If only they could see her now.

I HAVE MANY MEMORIES OF MY FATHER

BY ALEXANDRA BURT

Loomis, CA, 1975

The barn is still standing. Leaning, but standing. I won't set foot in it.

What I recall is that my father walked into that barn after all the scrap metal and farm machinery had been picked up. I remember the sun was a nearly perfect sphere in the sky. With his hat in hand, as if he was leaving church on Sunday morning, I watched my father emerge a different man. His farm was no longer.

I return on the day of my father's funeral. The finest chestnut wood was used to construct his coffin. As the chestnut ages, its bark hardens with every passing year. Furrows twist around the trunk, making it look malformed, warped and unpredictable. One can never be sure what direction the cable-like strands will take.

As I stand in front of the farmhouse, my heels dig into the dirt as if to brace myself for what's coming. I realize how easily we slip back within the four walls of our childhood and I turn into a little girl, sitting on the wooden steps leading up to the front door, drawing stick figures in the dust. The house looks the same: a modest, no-frills building with lots of exposed wood and little, if any, ornamentation. Maybe it got a new roof and possibly the steps have been replaced, but I can't be sure, it's been too long. Thirty-five years is an entire lifetime.

The ceiling, held up by weathered wooden beams, is covered in discolored patches from water leaks. I recall little of the living room. The walls, once painted in vibrant blue hues, have faded over time, revealing layers of the past through cracked and peeling paint. The fireplace is still there. Large and made of stone, it dominates the wall. A collection of vintage photographs and heirlooms sit on the mantel. The creaking wooden floor-boards underfoot groan with the weight of generations. Sunlight filters through the curtains, casting a glow on the worn leather armchair by the window. Next to it, a small table with an old transistor radio.

We listened to President Roosevelt every night. There were things I couldn't explain, but I understood everybody was making sacrifices. Mine was wearing clothes with patches and mended socks. One day, we gathered in the living room. Daniel and I had settled on the couch while my mother sat silently at the nearby kitchen table, mending the clothes we had torn up during the week. Her back was straight, her legs crossed at the ankles. Concentrating on a hole in one of my skirts, she glanced up at my father's coffee mug. She abandoned her work and filled his mug with coffee, cream, and sugar. My father sat in a chair and on that scratchy Astor radio. FDR's voice spoke of "inevitable triumph" as his gaze drifted off into the distance. He turned the knob, and the radio concluded with a resisting howl. "I've decided to turn this place into a rabbit farm," he said.

"A rabbit farm?" I asked while fidgeting on the couch. "Do we get to play with the rabbits?"

"No, Ruby," my father said and unfolded the newspaper. "There'll be rules."

"Rules?" I asked and looked at Daniel.

"Yeah, what rules?" Daniel chimed in, flipping through a leather-bound edition of the *Atlas of the World*.

I pulled my feet up on the old, worn couch and scooted closer to him. I glimpsed the newest edition of *Women's Illustrated* in between the atlas pages. On the front cover of the magazine was a woman in a white bathing suit aboard a cruise ship named Neptune. "Your New Beach Frock," printed in large letters, obscured her thighs.

I giggle at the thought of my father catching him looking at pictures of briefs and women's girdles.

"I've done research on the matter," my father said, throwing a stern look at me. "We'll be raisin' American Blues. That's what the breed's called. They fetch a hefty price at the furrier in town. And the rules are: the rabbits are a means of getting by. No funny business, you understand?" A long speech about the fixed ratio of does and bucks followed this, and their rapid growth rate. "Farm animals are property, worth the meat on their bones, and the fur on their back. Remember that," he added.

"We can't play with them? Can we give them names, at least?" Daniel insisted.

My father rose and stretched his limbs. Every time he moved, he had to negotiate his body's movements as if he was bending joints against their will. Sometimes, after a lot of rain, he winced. "No names. And we only breed the bluest ones for the pelts," my father said, towering over us.

Daniel had watched him closely and slammed shut the atlas in his lap. Their eyes met in the dim light of the room, and something passed between them. Did my father see the magazine in Daniel's lap? I couldn't say what it was, but there was an exchange between them. A subtle shift in energy.

I abandon the living room. The kitchen is organized, there is nothing here for me to see. I hesitate. The smell of rabbits still hangs in the air. Once the rabbit operation was in full swing, my mother prepared rabbit meat in so many ways that it could pass for chicken, pork, and sometimes even beef. She served it baked or fried, as stew, casserole, sausage, pot pie. Even rabbit on a stick.

I don't remember going hungry once, even during the Great Depression, but food was the furthest from my mind. My father became prone to violent outbursts. We avoided eye contact, never held his gaze, and we never took the last rabbit's leg until we were sure he would not claim it. Was it the war, was it the rabbits, or was it us? We never could tell. There wasn't much my father liked, but a lot he hated—the Japanese, the Germans, and the Jews—but Marlene Dietrich left him livid. Her voice on the radio made him hit the off button with a jerky movement. She wore a man's clothes, and she was loose, he said. We didn't know what that meant, but what we knew was that if we completed our chores with lightning speed, we got to spend forbidden time with the rabbits. Not all of them, but the two Daniel had picked out. He named them *True* and *Blue* because their pelts were of the deepest sapphire.

One day, upstairs in our room, where we laid low after we had spent an hour with the rabbits, we schemed. Over the years, I'd come back to that moment, realizing it meant different things to us: to me it was a prank, for Daniel, an act of mutiny.

"If we ever call them by their names, by mistake, he won't notice because he'll think we're talking about the breed. If you don't squeal, he'll never know." Daniel stared at the ceiling. "Stupid rule anyway," he added. "We have hundreds of rabbits. You'd think he could spare a couple. We're not asking for something impossible, right?"

"You know how he is and how everything makes him mad since he hurt his leg and he can't fight in the war," I said. Hurting his leg was too mild an expression to explain the way the skin was taut and shiny, stretching over his knee. He was careless out in the barn, my mother told us, but never told us the specifics.

"He is a cripple," Daniel said. A pause. Then "he kills rabbits, you know," he added.

"For pelts and food," I replied. But my heart sank.

"Not those. The others."

"What others?"

Daniel paused for a moment. "The ones that don't look right. He kills the ones that are... different, I guess. The wrong color, crooked teeth, too small. I've seen it. He drowns them. In a bucket."

I didn't know how to respond. In my mind's eye, I could see a bucket full of hairless, toothless rabbits, spilling over the pails' rims.

"I've seen it. More than once," Daniel insisted. "I hate him and how he treats the rabbits. And how he never lets us get away with anything, and always..." Daniel didn't finish the sentence and walked over to the window.

"Tonight's Halloween," I said to distract him, "if there's any day of the year we can get away with anything, it's Halloween."

Together we lay down on our beds and stared at the ceiling, weighing our options. "Don't play with the animals," he said, mocking my father's voice. Daniel snickered, but only for a second, then his face went blank. "Here's what we're going to do," he added in a whisper.

I listened intently.

~

That night, I slipped a toy gun into my father's old tool belt. I put on a vest I found in the attic and as I attached a shiny belt buckle; the outfit was all but complete. If a woman in men's clothes was what my father hated most, a female sheriff was the most scandalous thing I could imagine. I slipped on my boots and stepped out of my room. My mother, at the bottom of the stairs, was shaking a Ray-O-Vac flashlight, but couldn't figure out how to turn it on. My father wore his usual overalls and his old straw hat. He looked more like a scarecrow than a crippled farmer.

"Don't make a wrong move now or I'll throw you in jail, ya hear?" I shouted as my mother juddered the flashlight. She pointed it towards her face as it came to life. My father looked me up and down but didn't say a word. The flashlight's beam cast an eerie glow around the house as Daniel appeared. He descended the stairs like a blushing bride on her wedding day, slowly, step by step, holding a flower bouquet made entirely from white wrapping paper. He had draped an old bed sheet around his body, gathered by a rope around his waist and accessorized with a hat and my mother's church shoes.

My mother gasped and dropped the flashlight. My father stared at Daniel, a blue rope of fury pushing through his temples. I took in a deep breath and started humming the wedding march. My father waved his right fist at Daniel. I recognized that certain flinch in his eyes, the one that was always followed by a beating that left you unable to remember your own name. Daniel ran past us and out the front door, taking the porch steps as if he was going for first base, steering toward flashlights and lanterns coming up our driveway.

I had never seen my father trying to run. He waddled more than he sprinted, like a faulty mechanism, unable to gain speed or maintain any kind of dignity. The neighbors stood in awe as a limping farmer in overalls chased a twelve-year-old boy bride, veil flowing in midair, the straw-hat limp on the ground.

In the kitchen, a bitter scent is nipping at my nose. All those decades, all those rabbit dishes, yet a putrid trace hangs about this kitchen. Is it the burnt pancakes my mother made the morning after Halloween? Downstairs, the biting scent of a plate of burnt pancakes greeted me in the middle of the kitchen table. I inspected both sides of the pancakes and picked the lightest one.

"They're outside," my mother said, almost spilling the milk as she poured me a glass. "It's been a long time."

I didn't catch on at first, but then everything that moved stood still. "Both of them?" I asked. "Outside."

"Outside," she repeated, and her eyes filled with tears.

My mother made as much noise as she could, rearranging dishes in the sink, but nothing could drown out what I heard next. A high-pitched yelp came from the barn, echoing all the way to the marrow of my bones, followed by a primal scream. I felt the blood settle into the lower half of my body. The pancake in my mouth solidified. I sat still and waited for the next thing to happen.

My mother opened one of the lower cabinets and took out a large roaster, the one reserved for Thanksgiving turkeys and Christmas ducks. The slamming back door startled both of us. Daniel walked in. He didn't have any visible injuries, no bloody lip, no bruised eye. He neither limped nor walked funny the way he did when our father put a serious stick or belt to him. He slid his right side on a chair and then carefully followed with the rest of his body, tucking his hands under his thighs.

"Get ready for church," my mother said. We did as we were told.

~

During church service, Daniel stared straight ahead. Even my parents didn't look at each other. Every time someone coughed, dropped a hymnal, or the wooden pews screeched, Daniel flinched. After church, my parents shook hands with the pastor while Daniel and I waited in the car. The drive home was silent.

The house greeted us with an aroma of rosemary and gravy. We took off our coats and boots and sat at the kitchen table. Mom took the roaster out of the oven, scooped potatoes and carrots in a bowl, and sat the pot in the middle of the table. There lay two rabbits; hogtied, hind legs bound with twine, cavities stuffed with thyme, rosemary, apples, and sage.

The helpless terror I felt, the hate that hatched inside of me, as I heard myself speak. "You killed our rabbits?" My voice didn't sound like me at all. I felt tempted to whisper something in Daniel's ear, something about our father being broken and us picking other rabbits, but what would be the point? Daniel's head seemed too heavy for him to hold up. I had never seen my brother like this before, his skin blotchy, his eyes dark and feverish.

"Eat. Everybody eat." My father's voice was low and steady, but carried the fury of a tornado.

We picked up our forks and did as we were told.

~

There is one lingering memory I have thought of often over the years. One day, a litter of rabbits were born. Their spines were soft and their heads seemed too large for their bodies. All six of them were missing their rib cages. Daniel put them in a box, fed them with milk from an eyedropper. Even so, all of them died within hours.

My father was a man of few words, never one to dwell on anything but the work that was required to run the farm. We talked about the weather, about radio shows and the spore disease of the runner beans. The health of the rabbits was not something he dwelled on. He told us that a bad batch was part of life and those were the rules and rules can't be ignored. The day the malformed rabbits died, Daniel and I dug a hole behind the barn and buried them. Our father watched us fill the hole with dirt and stood between us afterwards. Daniel and I were uncomfortable. When we fidgeted, our father jerked as if he was going to put his arms around our shoulders, but then thought otherwise. I wonder what thought left this gesture unfinished, but he stood between us as if allowing us to tether ourselves to his way of thinking. I have many memories of my father, but that's my favorite memory of him. I guess both things can be true at the same time.

By the time of the funeral, my mother has passed and my brother is no longer with us. I stand alone, staring at the flowers covering his chestnut coffin. The wood is reddish brown with variations in color and grain, smooth and polished. How would they feel about him today, I wonder? I can only speak for myself. Once I left the farm, it felt as if my bones shifted. But not one story is simple. Not one story is complete. What I know is that my father was smart for a man in overalls and the rabbit farm kept us from going hungry during the war. His rules were his way of creating bricks out of chaos and building survival. The war made a peculiar man out of him and

I learned war wounds take on many forms, even far away from the battlefield.

How does one heal? Exposed to the sun, they say, scars darken. I can't speak for Daniel, but my wounds healed clean. No raised marks, no discolored skin. Just a slight pulling and tugging on a rainy day.

PART II

IF THERE BE ONE, TRY AND FIND IT

We think that monsters are banished to the dark. We tell ourselves that nightlights protect us and keep the demons in the shadows. We hope that the moon, the sun's complement, will reflect enough sunlight to keep us safe or guide our way. We tell ourselves that it's just the wind, a tree bumping against a windowpane. Once the sun rises, we'll see that it's nothing. All will be well.

But the sun doesn't protect us. It only reveals the truth.

There are always monsters among us.

Ashes to ashes,
Dust to dust,
Scorching embers,
Dresses like rust.

A blazing sun
Pounds the land.
A mother's love
Makes a demand.

They find enemies,
Bold and strong,
They fight the fight
And right the wrongs.

There's a price to pay
For what you've done.
For every evil
Under the sun.

VP Chandler

EMBER EYES
BY VP CHANDLER

"Lord, what's that smell?"

Roscoe and Elias reined in their horses. Elias pushed his straw hat higher on his forehead and lifted his nose in the air. "Smells like somethin' dead. C'mon." He nudged his horse and followed the stench. He expected it was a dead deer or cow—not an uncommon sight in the rocky hills west of San Antonio. "Hope it's just a deer. We got a lot of work to do today."

Roscoe muttered a noncommittal answer.

Elias chuckled to himself. Roscoe could be good company, but he had an aversion to unpleasant things, such as work.

It was still early. The morning sun hadn't risen above the live oaks, but the dark blue morning twilight was enough to navigate. Even if it were dark, Elias wouldn't have needed the light. His nose told him where to go. Faithful Roscoe lagged a few minutes behind, apparently not eager to find whatever the stench was coming from.

Elias heard a shuffling near the bushes. and walked his horse closer. Black, hulking figures scuffled and hopped in the shadows. Elias flashed back to a childhood memory that never stayed buried for long: he and his father had been on their way to town when they came upon a massacred family. It had been blazing hot. The stench and images were imprinted in his five-year-old mind. The vultures' flapping wings brought him back to the present, and he shivered from a cold sweat. *Get ahold of yourself, old man. No more Comanches 'round here.* He urged his horse forward and saw what had attracted the birds. He shivered again.

Roscoe arrived a minute later as the sun peeked over the trees. He recoiled and covered his mouth with the crook of his arm. "Oh, my lord. Who'd do such a god-awful thing?"

Elias peered down at the corpse and knew who she was. He turned away, removed his hat, and wiped his brow. How much could one take in this life? He'd seen a lot in his sixty-five years —too much. How much bloodshed and heartache? Between skirmishes with Comanches, fighting Mexican troops, and losing his family to Yellow fever back in '67, he'd seen enough to last several lifetimes. Young men who were eager to test their mettle had no sense of what a toll violence can take. He knew what bullets, fire, knives, sabers could do to a body—. And to the mind of living witnesses. All the fight had left him long ago. He rarely raised his voice even when giving orders on the ranch. But violence seemed to find him, no matter how remote the place.

Despite his experiences, he'd never seen anything like what appeared before him now. Elias braced himself, covered his nose with the wild rag hanging around his neck. *Lord, give me strength to do right by this girl.* He dismounted. His knees almost buckled, but he stayed upright. Between the elements and the scavengers, the beauty of the young woman had been devastated—her eyes were now empty, blackened sockets. The contrast of her pale skin to the dark pits gave her even more of a ghoulish appearance.

Elias turned away and looked up at Roscoe. "I think we found Ruth Barnett." Everyone in the area knew that the beautiful young woman had been missing.

"My word!" Roscoe coughed to cover a sob, then he muttered a prayer.

Elias thought that the best thing he could do for the girl was to read the scene, same as he would when a predator had killed a calf, or as he had earlier in his life when he hunted the enemy. He stepped back. Her dress was disheveled, exposing her knees. Elias gently pulled the hem down to her ankles. He didn't want to think about what her condition was under the skirt. "She's been missin' for two days. I'd say that about goes with the state of her body. Wouldn't you say?"

"Lord, now how'd I know such a thing?"

Elias nodded and rubbed his grizzled chin. He knew. He was talking himself through the scene. He pointed to a bruise on her neck and leaned closer. "Looks like she mighta been choked. Not by a rope, something thinner."

Roscoe stayed on his horse. "My god, Elias. I cain't look." He focused on the eastern horizon as the sun rose higher above the trees. He squeaked, "Are her eyes et out?"

Elias studied her and the ground. "The critters have been at her some, but it looks like the eyes were burned out first." Nearby were the remnants of a campfire. "Probably with a stick from that fire over yonder." A strip of color near the fire pit caught his eye, and he bent down to pick up a red velvet ribbon that matched her dress. *Something thin, like a rope.* He put it in his pocket and returned to the young woman.

"Well, isn't that the kinda thing Comanches do? Burn out the eyes and such?"

Elias shook his head. "They're all on those reservations up north now. And from the tracks I'm seein', I'd say one man did this."

Roscoe ventured another look. "I cain't imagine that her ma bought that dress for her. It's fancy, like for a city girl. And I don't think I ever seen her in red. She always favored blue or green."

"Can we get back to helping this poor girl?"

Roscoe shuddered. "Elias, let's git."

Elias covered her with branches to keep the birds off, then remounted his horse. "Let's get back to the ranch. Mr. Warren'll notify her folks and the sheriff. And we can come back with a wagon."

He gave the girl one last look and wished he had a blanket to cover her. Nothing about the mutilated, eyeless young woman was the Ruth Barnett he watched grow up for the last eighteen years. Morning birdsong caught his attention, and he looked up. He wiped his eyes and surveyed the rugged landscape. Cedar and sagebrush could take hold and grow in rock, survive the extreme elements. It was beautiful and harsh. And though it was hard on a body, people could also thrive. Someone had taken that away from Ruth. They had put the poor girl through hell, and he hoped that he could help catch the animal that hurt her.

When Elias returned and informed the Warrens, Mrs. Warren shoved one of her quilts into his hands. "Something to cover her with." A white blanket with a blue and canary yellow wedding ring pattern. He'd seen it many times over the years. He knew it had been a wedding gift to the Warrens. And he'd seen the girls use it as a blanket for pretend tea parties on the front porch, or they had bundled themselves in it on the porch swing.

"That's kind of you. But, pardon me for saying, you won't be able to use it again. Considering her condition."

Her look could have turned a charging bull away. "You take a wagon and bring that girl back here, covered, like decent folk. James will send word to her parents and the sheriff."

"Yes, ma'am." He held the blanket and looked down upon her. Mrs. Warren, Amanda, whom he had watched grow from a reticent girl to a strong woman. He had given her "horsie rides" on his back, taught her how to tie knots, and wrangle horses. Things that a father or uncle should teach. Her laughter had once been a stab in his heart but also the balm that he had needed at the lowest time in his life. She healed him. He was proud of the woman she had become. He sometimes wondered if she knew how dear she was to him. She wasn't his daughter, but he felt like she was.

Elias took two men and returned a couple of hours later after retrieving Ruth and navigating the rocky hills. When he finally made it to the ranch, the sun was at high noon and warming up the body. He saw from a distance that Sheriff Lowe and the Barnett's were waiting with the Warren family. As he drew closer, he could see that the Barnett's were fidgeting and anxious. He figured they were hoping it wasn't their daughter. Any parent would be hoping the same. Elias knew that dread all too well. Another memory to bury.

Mr. Barnett put an arm around his wife. She sagged, stood up, then wiped her nose with a white handkerchief. Both Warren daughters, Lillie and Sallie, stood by their parents. Lillie had been Ruth's best friend. And like Ruth Barnett, she had grown into a beauty. Sallie, at eight, hadn't reached her coltish phase yet.

Elias parked the wagon on a knoll, downwind from the house. His companions exited the wagon and left him to his task.

Mrs. Warren seemed irritated and motioned for him to come nearer. He shook his head, and she slowly lowered her arm, catching his meaning. Better to stay downwind.

He glanced towards the bunkhouse as the other cowhands filed onto the low, wooden porch. He had never seen them so quiet. Most had watched Ruth and Lillie play on the ranch over the years. All were fond of the girls who had grown into lovely and kind-hearted young women. Strangers often mistook them for sisters, and the girls would happily play along, saying they were twins. They were born the same year and had the same striking blue eyes, but while Ruth had had golden hair, Lillie's was chestnut.

The sheriff and Mr. Warren crossed the yard, kicking up puffs of dust along the way. The summer had been brutal, and the grass was yellow-brown. Mr. Warren strode with purpose. Elias knew that he was a man who liked to think he was in charge. It was clear that the sheriff wasn't in a hurry. He was older, and, like Elias, he'd probably seen enough death to know that things were dealt with in their own time.

Elias didn't move to uncover her. "Do her folks know her condition?"

Mr. Warren said, "We thought it best to reveal the tragedy a bit at a time, so we withheld a few painful details. They know it's probably her and that she met with some sort of foul play."

Elias rubbed his chin. "I suggest we keep them from lookin'. No parent needs to see this."

Mr. Warren glanced at the sheriff, and they nodded. "Perhaps that's prudent."

Sheriff Lowe walked to the rear of the wagon bed. "Usually, we have someone from the family identify a body. But seeing as how you two knew her well enough, I'd have no problem if y'all did it."

Mr. Warren hesitated and then nodded. Elias pulled himself into the wagon and unfolded just enough of the blanket to reveal her face. Mr. Warren recoiled and covered his mouth and nose with his hand.

Mrs. Barnett called out across the barren yard, "Is it her? Is it my Ruth?"

Mr. Warren held up his hand to signal "just a moment." He moved in closer and said in a low voice, "Lord, have mercy. I thought I was prepared. Poor child." He turned to the crowd and nodded.

Mrs. Barnett howled and collapsed to the ground. Mr. Barnett knelt by her and held her. Even across the yard Elias saw the man shaking from grief.

Lillie Warren ran up the wooden porch steps, into the limestone house, and slammed the screen door. Mrs. Warren attended to the grieving parents while Sallie picked up her cat and sat on the porch.

The sheriff looked at Ruth again and mumbled to himself, "Hmm, odd."

"It's more than odd. It's horrific," Warren blurted.

The sheriff cleared his throat. "Yes, of course. Um, may I confide in you gentlemen?"

Elias was ashamed of himself for feeling prideful at such a moment. But he had never been called a gentleman before. He hopped down from the wagon and glanced in the direction of the house. Mrs. Warren had moved the Barnetts inside.

The sheriff continued. "This is not the first time I've encountered a young woman with eyes burned out and clad in some sort of dark red dress. In fact, there've been many in San Antonio. It's something that the lawmen in the area have been trying to solve for years now. At first it was once a year, but in the past couple of years it's happened more often. We're all eager to catch this killer. Perhaps he knew this and moved to more isolated environs. I must admit that this is the first gal from a good family. And she's the first young woman with blonde hair."

Mr. Warren raised his voice. "I have connections in town. Why haven't I heard of this?"

The sheriff pursed his lips. "Do you care what happens to ladies of the evening? To servant girls?"

Mr. Warren stood straight. "Are you implying that Ruth was—"

The sheriff raised a hand. "I'm implying no such thing. But the fiend—or fiends—who have done this have chosen those women for a reason. To attack a family girl like Ruth is bold."

Elias asked, "Were they also choked with something like a small, thin rope?"

The sheriff seemed surprised. "Why yes. You've a keen eye for detail. A matching red ribbon was often left around the necks of the victims."

"Like this one?" He pulled out the ribbon he had found by the fire.

"Exactly."

Elias tried to give it to the sheriff, but he refused. "I've a collection already."

Elias nodded and studied it again. He was holding the ribbon that had been in the killer's hands. The ribbon that had strangled the life from sweet Ruth Barnett. Unsure what to do with it, he returned it to his pocket. "Why the eyes, Sheriff? Why does he, um, burn out the eyes?"

"Well now, on that account we have some information. Just a few months ago one of his victims escaped. Poor girl was able to tell us some of how he thinks. He said, "When I kill you, my Anna will come back to me. She'll see through your eyes. Moments later, when he turned away to stoke the fire, the girl escaped."

"Thank god," said Mr. Warren.

The sheriff nodded. "Indeed. It's not much, but anything may help us. I think we have a better understanding of him. We're looking into who this 'Anna' could be."

Mr. Warren said, "Let's hope that Ruth is the last to suffer such a fate."

All the men agreed.

Elias sat in his wooden "thinking" chair at the base of the large oak in the yard near the bunkhouse. He always felt the spot to be representative of who he was, the link between the house and the hands. He also liked this time of day, at sunset, when one begins to wind down and think upon the day's events. But he knew there would be no rest tonight.

He pulled on a cigarette and let the hot smoke caress his mouth and throat. It calmed him. He pushed the morning's scene from his mind and needed to pace. When he stood, he could see through the dining room window to where the Warrens were eating dinner. He couldn't hear the conversation but knew the family well, so he could imagine what they were saying. Mr. Warren ate and motioned for a second pour of whiskey. Lillie picked at her food and often touched the silver sun pendant she wore on a chain. Mrs. Warren, probably trying to make small talk, as she was raised to do. The youngest, Sallie, eyed the rest of the family as she ate. She looked lost.

He wanted to scoop her up in his arms and promise to protect her. Life had taught him at a young age that innocence could be lost too soon. How many nights had he stayed awake in bed waiting to hear the footfalls of Comanches coming to kill his family? Or the hardship of surviving months away from home, killing men—for what? Freedom? He'd never be free when haunted by events and faces of the past.

As he moved away from the window he looked back once more. Mrs. Warren's brown hair was the same as Sallie's. The same as—he pushed the thought away, then let himself feel the pain. Like an aching joint that needed to be rubbed.

He felt worn down by death. The same brown hair as his daughter, Emily. And to think Emily, if she had lived, would be Mrs. Warren's age. Through the years he'd do the math, imagining the time markers: *she'd be getting married about now*, or, *I'd be a grandpa about now*. Sometimes Sallie took on Emily's likeness when the light hit just right. Later, the demons would be after him. When his mind caved in on itself—all that death. Over time it got to where it all seemed like too much.

He'd killed rattlesnakes and would do what needed to be done on the ranch. But reckless, random killing, even the smallest animal seemed cruel to him. But he never let on about it. He knew he'd be ridiculed. Most cowhands are young men, and they don't know how each death can get stacked on one another until it weighs you down.

Once he had to track and kill a rabid coyote. When he found it, he studied it through the mesquites. It was ambling back and forth as if it were drunk. It wasn't the coyote's fault that it was suffering. He knew he was doing it a favor by putting it out of its misery before the disease progressed even further. But even that was hard. He shot it and, as it was dying, he approached, tears blurring his vision. "I'm sorry. I'm sorry." When it finally died, he wept for over an hour. Why he'd cry so much over a coyote, he had no idea. He buried it. Saying words over an animal's grave seemed foolish, so he stood in silence and listened to the bugs and birds. It seemed the right thing to do. His idea of God had changed over the years—how could it not? And as he got older, he realized that life, beauty, and innocence were gifts to be protected.

So tonight, he'd stay by his thinking oak and keep an eye out to protect the people who had been the only family he'd known for decades.

The dining room was dark now. There was lamplight coming from the upstairs bedrooms and firelight from Mr. Warren's study. Elias tightened his lips. Surely Mr. Warren would ease up on the whiskey tonight. His family may need him.

The front door opened, and Mrs. Warren gently closed the screen door. She stepped into the moonlight, "Evening, Elias. I think I see you in your chair."

He stood and approached. "Evening, Miss Amanda." He sometimes used her given name when he was feeling nostalgic.

She smiled. "It's been a long time since you've called me that. What are you doing out here in the dark, playing guard dog?"

"Yes, ma'am."

"And we're happy to have you. How long have you been with us now?"

He stepped onto the porch. "Well, first your father and now you. I believe comin' on somethin' like thirty years."

"Oh, my lord."

Elias chuckled. "I think you've spent too much time around Roscoe."

She smiled. "He's a tender soul, isn't he?"

"I suppose so. Though he could be a little less tender when it comes to work."

They laughed. She said, "I suppose every ranch has a Roscoe. He's always been good with the girls, like you were with me. And he's taught Cook a thing or two. He helps in lots of ways." Her smile fell and she wrung her hands. "What's happened is a horrible business. I'm worried about my girls." She looked into Elias's eyes.

He had a knot in his throat. He wanted to put his arms around her and protect her. "Yes, ma'am."

They sat in a pair of porch chairs.

She patted his hand. "I'm glad you're here. We've always been able to count on you. You're like family."

"Thank you, ma'am."

"Now, Elias. Enough of this "ma'am" nonsense. When I say you're like family, you're family. I wish you'd not be so distant."

"Thank you, Miss Amanda. Just doing what's proper."

"In some ways you've been more like a father to me than my own. You're dear to us. I hope you know that."

He cleared the lump that was in his throat and didn't respond.

They were quiet with their own thoughts for a few minutes. Then Mrs. Warren whispered, "Elias, I'm worried about Lillie. I feel that there's something that I'm not seeing. I haven't told James, but Ginny Barnett thinks that Ruth had a secret beau. She had been acting as young, smitten women do. Smiling and humming, keeping to herself more. If Lillie had a secret beau, would I know? I thought I'd know. But she's been different, more guarded lately."

"You're doin' a good job, Miss Amanda. Just keep 'em close. I'll keep my eyes open, too." He pulled the ribbon from his pocket and showed her. "Does this look familiar to you?"

"No. Was Ruth wearing it?"

He nodded but said no more.

"Shouldn't the sheriff have that?"

He shook his head. "I tried to give it to him, but he said he's got plenty of 'em. See, this isn't the only occasion like this. It's been goin' on for a while, for years now."

"Oh, my—" her hands began to shake.

"I got a feelin' too."

After chatting for some time, Mrs. Warren went inside to retire for the evening and check on her girls one more time.

Elias rose from his chair and peeked into the window of the study. Mr. Warren was asleep in his polished leather chair, mouth agape. Tumbler empty, on the floor. Elias's gut twisted. He knew too well the habit of drinking to excess to numb pain and shock. And, as usual on the Warren ranch, Amanda Warren stayed strong, sober, and alert. He'd often heard her say under her breath, "Well, someone has to run things around here." He was always proud of her. And the best thing that he could do for her and the family was to stay alert.

Elias returned to his chair to keep watch. Sallie's bedroom light was out but Lillie's was still on. He assumed that Mrs. Warren was talking to her. What words of advice or comfort was she offering? What does one say to their daughter when their best friend was strangled, and her eyes burned out? He shuddered and stood up. The hairs on his neck prickled. He scanned the yard, listening. Nothing. He looked up at the window and saw Mrs. Warren looking down at him. He stepped into the light, and she motioned for him to come up.

He quietly hopped onto the porch and went into the house, standing in the entry hall to listen. The house was quiet. He ascended the stairs as quietly as he could, thankful for the carpet runners—he didn't want to frighten Sallie. Although he'd only been on the second floor a handful of times to help move furniture, he knew which door was Lillie's. Mrs. Warren was standing in the doorway. "What is it?" he whispered.

"I don't know how to explain it. But when the lamplight flickered, I swear I saw someone standing in Lillie's closet."

"Mama, you're being crazy. There's no one there."

Mrs. Warren didn't acknowledge Lillie. She looked into Elias's eyes. "Can you look, please?" She handed him the lamp.

"Of course." He stepped into the bedroom. Lillie was sitting in bed in her nightgown, the covers pulled up to her chin.

"Evenin', Miss Lillie."

"Evening, Elias. Mama's being silly. There's nothing in the closet and I'd like to try to get some sleep now."

"Yes, ma'am. But I think we'd all feel better if I took a quick look."

Lillie started to protest again but a snap of her mother's fingers shut her down.

The flicker of the light made the corner shadows dance. A feeling flashed through him, and he imagined he was approaching a doorway to a nightmare. *Don't be silly. It's just a girl's closet.* With dread, he took that first step and felt a prickle on his neck again. He'd felt that was more than once when he'd been near a rattlesnake but didn't know until it rattled.

He shined the light into the closet. So much fabric—so many dresses for one girl. He wished that they were shorter so he could get a clearer view of the floor. He gently swatted at the dresses and moved them around to see if anything was on the floor.

There was an odor that seemed out of place. It seemed like a hint of cologne, sour sweat, and smoke. Was it him? He knew fear had a smell. He quickly batted at the dresses and began to turn to the women to offer comforting words, then froze. Something had caught his eye.

"Elias? What's wrong?" Mrs. Warren took a step closer to the closet doorway.

Lillie's voice rose. "There's nothing in there. Come on out."

Elias stared at Mrs. Warren, too afraid to look at what he thought he'd seen. He made himself turn to the dresses in the back of the closet and held up the lamp. A sliver of dark red peeked from behind a bright yellow dress. He moved the dresses aside and lifted the red dress by the hanger. He held it out for Mrs. Warren to see.

She gasped and her eyes widened in horror. She pivoted and faced Lillie. "Lillie Marianna Warren. You'd better start talking."

"Please, Mama, don't' be mad! I'm in love."

Elias hung the dress back on the rod and stepped out of the closet. He wasn't sure if he should be there. This was a conversation between and mother and daughter.

Mrs. Warren said, "Lillie M—"

"Ruth and I had matching dresses!"

Mrs. Warren took a deep breath.

Lillie continued, rubbing the sun pendant that rested on her chest.

"Darling, why do you have matching dresses?"

Elias saw that Mrs. Warren's knuckles were white from squeezing the bed post.

"Because that's what he wanted. He gave them to us. Just like he gave me this necklace."

Elias thought he heard movement in the closet.

"Lillie, darling, you need to get to the heart of the matter."

Lillie hesitated. "Please don't be mad. But this is an engagement present. We're going to be wed. I promise you he's a good man and he loves me."

Mrs. Warren shouted, "Tell me who he is!"

Words tumbled out of Lillie. "Ruth and I met him in town. He's ever so nice. I know he couldn't have hurt Ruth! He said that my name 'Lillie Marianna' was even a sign, even though he liked Ruth's eyes better."

Mrs. Warren leaned over the bed and grabbed Lillie by the arms. "Would a good man torture a girl and burn out her eyes?"

Lillie gasped. "No!"

Dresses erupted from the closet and a man ran past Elias and out the door. One garment got tangled in Elias' feet and he fell. He recovered in a few seconds, but the man was already down the stairs.

Mrs. Warren shouted something Elias didn't understand.

Elias heard the front door slam shut. He pursued. Lillie wailed upstairs. He reached the front door and stopped—he didn't know if the man was armed. He knew that Mr. Warren kept a Colt in his desk, so he ran to the study. Mr. Warren was still asleep and drooling in his chair. Elias grabbed the gun and a handful of extra bullets and stuffed them into his pockets.

He stood on the front porch and listened. A horse galloped out through the front gate. He ran towards it and saw pale puffs of dust in the moonlight as the man rode away. Elias turned towards the stables to saddle a horse. But a horse nicker by the house caught his attention. Another horse was tethered to a tree. It must have been saddled for Lillie. His heart fell. How close had they been to losing her, too? How had he not noticed?

He jumped on the horse and galloped down the road in pursuit, thankful for a bright moon. Would the man continue on the road or go off trail? He slowed and listened. Nothing. He felt like a fool chasing after a killer into the night by himself. But it certainly wasn't the first time he'd hunted by moonlight. He sniffed the air. Dust hadn't settled yet. The man had ridden the horse through here at a full pace.

He did the same as he thought about his quarry. Most of the killings had been in the city. He thought about the explosion of clothes from the closet. Did he see anything of the man? And his victims were dressed in finery. So, he's likely a city man who has money. Chances are he'll stay on the road until he reaches more familiar territory.

Elias pursued at a full gallop while keeping an eye for puffs of dust off the road. And what was the plan? Would he capture him and take him to the sheriff? If possible, he would.

After a couple of miles, something to his right caught his attention, a flicker in the moonlight on a distant hill. He slowed his horse and walked to the shadow of a mesquite tree. If Elias could see the enemy, the man could possibly see him. He dismounted, tied the horse to the tree, and proceeded on foot. Elias knew there was a cave nearby. Perhaps the man had learned a bit about the local landscape. Afterall, he had killed

Ruth a couple of days ago. He'd have had plenty of time to find a place to hide. He could have also set up traps.

Elias proceeded with caution. He crept, listened, then ran to hide behind a bush. He heard a horse clear its nose. It was near the cave. He listened. Was the man in the cave or was it a trap? He waited in the dark.

A crunch of footsteps in the distance to his left caught his attention. Elias strained his eyes. There it was—something, a silhouette in the dark. He had been right. The cave had been a ruse. He looked towards the figure. He saw the flash of light, then heard the gunshot and unmistakable whiz go by him. He fired off a few of his own shots in the man's direction.

He had been here before, more than once. He hoped experience would give him an edge. He called out, "Might as well give yourself up." Then he scrambled into the shade of nearby brush. Maybe the man's ego would give him away. Elias waited.

Another gunshot but where Elias had been standing. Good. The man can be tricked. Elias moved to circle around. He occasionally threw a small rock in the opposite direction to keep the killer confused.

In no time Elias was on a slope, looking down at the man's back, perhaps sixty feet away. In the gray moonlight he could see that the man was a dandy, dressed for town, not the country. Elias shifted his weight and a small rock tumbled down the hill.

The man twirled around. Elias shot twice without thinking. The man collapsed. Elias ran to retrieve the gun before the man could fire again. He kicked aside the revolver and looked down on him. Two in the chest. He was both impressed and sickened that his aim was still accurate.

The man was clinging to life. He gurgled when he tried to speak. "Please."

"Please?" Elias leaned over him. The scent of sour sweat and cologne assailed his nose. "How many women begged you for their lives?" He shoved the man with his foot. "Huh? Why'd you do it?"

The man's eyes roamed around as if seeking a face. "They had my Anna's eyes. Anna was supposed to marry *me*. I wanted her forever. I bound us together with her blood. Her wedding dress turned a beautiful red." He smiled and tried to chuckle. "When I killed them, she came back to me. If only for a moment. Then she'd be gone. And then dead eyes, looking. I had to stop their stares. But I always needed to see her again."

Elias knew about glassy eyes accusing or seeing something only the dead could see. He was haunted by those stares too. He wanted to silence them. He reached into his pocket and fingered the ribbon. He thought of Ruth, and he itched to strangle the man with it.

The man wheezed. Blood pooled around him.

If he were a coyote, Elias would have put him out of his misery. He stood, looking down at the being at his feet. He'd seen people shot and struggling for breath, their lives seeping from them. His nightmares were full of such memories.

He pulled out the ribbon from his pocket and held it in front of the man's face. "What's your name? Just so's we know."

The man squinted and tried to focus. His eyes glimmered when he saw the ribbon. "John. Sanderson."

Elias gave it to him, stepped back and watched. He half-wondered if Anna or Ruth, or any of the other women would appear to wreak vengeance. He waited and listened until the gasping stopped. He sat in the silence and waited for that familiar emptiness he felt when someone died.

He sat in the darkness, lost in thought. Visions of blood, burning and mangled bodies, and staring eyes. Then a memory he thought had been long forgotten: His daughter's smile. Emily, pure sunshine and joy. It was a painful gift, but a gift none-theless. Around him, the oaks and brush now filled with the sounds of crickets and cicadas. Life. He thought about Amanda Warren, the girls, Roscoe, the cowhands, and even Mr. Warren. He'd known too much of death. Maybe it was time to allow himself some happiness, to step a little closer to them.

He stood and his knees complained. He dusted off his hat and turned to the east. A new day with the blue morning twilight forming. He heard the footfalls of a horse and watched the familiar silhouette crest the hill.

"Oh, Lord."

"Good to see you too, Roscoe."

SNAKES

BY VP CHANDLER

Summer on the Texas plains can be unbearable. Even while in the house the sun the blinds me, so I stay away from the open windows. Nary a breeze lifts the sheer curtains. The air in the house is oppressive. I roam around the house and recall the day that Noel brought me to the ranch. I was disheartened. The house needed work and the air was full of the odors of cow dung. When he saw me try to block the smells by covering my nose with the back of my hand, he laughed. He said it smelled like money to him and that I'd get used to it. I sniff the air. I suppose I have gotten used to it. I don't smell it anymore.

The house is quiet. It's midday and Molly is taking her nap. Mother Bradshaw, Noel's mother, is sleeping nearby too. I've always liked of the tradition of the siesta. It's a necessity in Texas. But my spirit is restless, and I can't sleep.

Molly stirs. I go to her room and look down into her crib. Poor thing. She's so hot that her baby-fine strands are plastered to her forehead. She puckers her face as if she'll wake. I can't bear the thought of her howls piercing the peaceful silence, so I coo at her and she calms down.

I hear the slither in the wall. An instant rage fills me. I don't expect Mother Bradshaw to wake from the sound. It's subtle. One would only hear it if they've heard it before, as I have, many, many times. It's maddening. I stand still and listen. It's in the wall of Molly's room. I pinpoint the source and put my ear to the wall, down near the floor. There it is again! Blast this cursed house. I've told Noel time and time again that rattlesnakes have gotten into the walls, but he never listens. He doesn't believe me. He "knows better because he's a man" and I'm not. How could a woman of nineteen years possibly know better than a man almost thirty? I survey all the floors to verify that there are no snakes outside of the walls and then rest in the parlor.

I spot a mother cow through the open window. She slowly chews her cud as her calf nurses. She turns and looks in my direction. If only it could be that simple. The talents of mother-hood and being a good wife seem to elude me.

I long to return to my childhood, a simpler time. But then I correct myself. No, those were not halcyon days. They were filled with their own troubles. I am not as pretty as my sisters. I'm quite plain, in fact. Boys showed no interest in a brown-haired girl with a wind-chapped face that stayed red from sneezing. I was never especially clever, but I'm not a simpleton either. I'm not tall and lithe as my sister Elaine. I'm not short and curvy like my friend Bella. In fact, I've always been too thin and somewhat sickly. One Saturday in Abilene, when everyone goes to town, I once overheard a stranger say to his sons, "Why, if she were a horse, I wouldn't buy her." They guffawed at the joke and walked away. I pretended not to hear but the barb hit its target and has been stuck ever since.

Mother Bradshaw's words still ring in my ears from the time Noel introduced me. They were in the entry and thought I couldn't hear. (Do people think I have no ears? Am I invisible?) Or perhaps she did not care. "Have you lost your wits? She's a plain girl with no promise. Look how sickly she is."

He declared, "She is the one for me, Mother." And that was that. The man had spoken.

I think my parents were relieved and happy to pay a small dowry as a wedding present. Knowing my father, he thought it would be a bargain in the end than to pay to take care of me for the rest of my life.

All seemed well in the beginning. I cooked and cleaned and kept a decent house. The wooden floors shined, and the white baseboards gleamed. And I'm a passable cook.

Then I saw the first rattlesnake. Of course, it was not the first rattlesnake I've ever seen. Anyone growing up in West Texas has seen their fair share of rattlers. But this one was invading my sanctuary. I was outside, fetching water. As I approached the front steps, movement to my left caught my eye. I saw its long body and rattle disappearing in the gap between the house footing and the wooden siding. I was so mad; I almost grabbed its tail and pulled it out. How dare he! But I thought the better of it. If I pulled it out, then what? It wasn't worth dying over. When I told Noel, he said I had a vivid imagination. I was flabber-gasted. I thought surely my husband would listen to me. Had I not taken good care of our home? "What about our safety?"

"We're fine. We're perfectly safe."

"But what about the baby?" I was not yet certain, for my body had never been predictable and seemed to follow its own timetable that I was never able to decipher. But I knew that changes were happening. And I thought that using the excuse of a child would possibly give me more leverage in my argument.

"Baby?" He turned to me and I saw a smile I had never seen before. Never in my entire life had someone shined a light on me. He treated me differently after that, but still insisted there were no snakes in the house.

As the months passed, I would hear them in the walls. At night, sleep eluded me. Many a night I spent with a lantern in hand, listening with my ear pressed to the boards. Inside the walls, it sounded like a hand sliding over paper. Why couldn't anyone else hear it? Knowing there was danger and impotent to prevent it was maddening.

Time progressed and the baby grew in my belly. I was nauseous every moment. How did other women "glow"? I lost all desire to eat. It was then that Mother Bradshaw moved into the spare room to keep me healthy. While Noel ran the ranch and did business in Abilene, more than a day's ride, Mother Bradshaw fed me and tended to the house. It would have helped if the woman could cook. How did Noel ever thrive in their home? I tried to be grateful and do my best. It was torturous and the following months did not help our marriage. But it was necessary for the sake of the baby.

And then my dear Molly was born. She came into the world absolutely perfect. Although she was beautiful, I saw the disappointment on Noel's face. His mother put her arm around him and said, "Next time." Of course he wanted a boy.

But I was happy. I had my beautiful Molly, and as the days went by, she grew only more marvelous. Somehow by God's grace she had green eyes like Noel's and not dull brown like mine. And her baby ringlets gave her a soft honey-colored halo. She was a beauty and the joy of my life. Again, by God's grace, my body was able to provide the needed nourishment. For we had all assumed that I was too thin to be able to. Molly is the one triumph in my life.

I now leave Molly's room and return to the parlor. The mother cow and calf now wander into the shade of a mesquite bush and rest. I feel a kinship with her more than any human I've ever encountered. She does not judge me. She does not sneer at my looks or bumbling attempts to be graceful. She eats, sleeps, and exists to provide for her offspring.

I'm surprised to see that sunlight now shines onto the parlor floor. How much time has passed? I don't know why I can't stand the patch of sunlight, but I do none the less. So I retreat to my bedroom to perhaps get some rest.

I pass by Molly's room. Mother Bradshaw is now awake, looking down at her, adjusting the bedding. I walk quietly to my bedroom. I know that neither of us wish to speak to each other. I lie on the bed and close my eyes. I'm restless. My mind flits from one thought to another. Molly, Noel, Mother Bradshaw, the sun, the heat, snakes hissing. I see an image of Noel laughing. I hear a hiss, open my eyes, and sit up. I listen again and hear nothing. I imagine Noel's smile and feel dread.

After Molly was born, he changed. His smiles no longer reached his eyes—a mask worn to fool me. Then the taunts began. One evening as I was clearing the table after supper, he tripped me as I walked by. But I was able to get my feet under me in time. Mother Bradshaw chided me for my clumsiness and Noel smirked. I was speechless. While he had never been an affectionate person, he had never treated me with animosity. That was the first of many small taunts and attacks. If I walked by, he'd pinch my arm or push or trip me. Mother Bradshaw never remarked.

One night while we lay in bed after retiring, I asked why.

"Don't be absurd. I love you just as much as the day we married." Then he ran a slow finger over my shoulder, collar bone, up my neck, over my lips, and crawled on top of me.

"I still feel as if I haven't healed properly after having the baby."

My protest fell on deaf ears. He did his will. Never had I felt like a vessel for his releases instead of a somewhat beloved wife.

I now dig the palms of my hands into my eyes to keep from crying. I'm trapped in this forsaken house on this remote ranch, married to a man who clearly does not want me. The heat, the smirks, the derision. I feel like I shall go mad. Molly is the only thing that gives me life.

A whinny of horses draws me to the dining room window. Mother Bradshaw is already on the porch to greet them. It's Noel escorting a young woman. She looks tidy but not too pretty. She's a bit stout and looks like she can handle chores. I'd wager she's a good worker. I feel my spirits lift; some domestic help would make my life easier, and Mother Bradshaw could move back into town.

They dismount their horses, and Mother Bradshaw steps into the yard. This irritates me. This is my household; I should be the one to greet her first. I walk onto the porch and at first the raging sun holds me back, but I step into the brightness anyway.

The trio walk the horses to the water trough under the shade tree. Noel wipes his brow. I hear a murmur of conversation and Noel smiles and says, "Yes." He seems to emphasize the "s," and lets it linger.

I draw closer. Her dress and hat are a bit worn. She doesn't come from money, but she's made an effort to be presentable.

A silk flower from the girl's hat is caught in the wind and lands in the trough. I suspect that what had once been a bright lemon yellow is now the color of pale lemonade.

It floats, then sinks.

A shiver stops me. Something's not right. My head swims. The heat, his smile, the trough, the girl, the yellow flower. It's wrong. A memory bubbles just under the surface. I feel ill.

The trough. Something about the trough.

And then I remember.

The blazing afternoon sun. Molly and Mother Bradshaw were asleep during siesta. Noel asked to speak with me out by the trough. "You are no longer needed or wanted."

"What do you mean?" How does a wife respond to such a

statement? What would become of me? Where would I go? What about Molly?

While I tried to grapple with understanding, he grabbed me by the throat and plunged my head under the water. I scratched at his hands and arms, flailing in my daisy-yellow cotton dress, my arms looking for some kind of purchase. They were too short to reach his face. My hands were too weak to break his grasp. I tried to grab the sides of the trough to pull myself up, but he was too heavy, too strong.

I was no match for him. Air left my lungs. My struggling ceased. The water calmed. In the last seconds of life, I looked at his face through the water. My husband, the man who promised to be my love and protector, the father of my child, was smiling. The smile finally reached his eyes.

I floated above the trough and looked down. I was surprised to see how slight I was below. How could such a pitiable thing hold a person's memories, desires, hopes? Odd that I thought my dress looked lovely as it wafted in the water.

He then positioned my whole body in the trough and placed a large rock in my arms. He practiced saying, "Yes. Poor thing. Couldn't handle motherhood."

Rage filled me as I floated above. I screamed but no one heard.

Now I hear Mother Bradshaw say to the girl, "Welcome, Mrs. Bradshaw."

I turn from the trough and see her arm around the young woman as they enter the house.

I follow. This girl, this poor creature. Will she eventually suffer the same fate as I? And what of my dear Molly?

"May I see the child?" she asks, as if reading my thoughts. "I love babies."

Dare I hope that kindness has entered this den of cruelty? I follow them.

Molly is waking and begins to fuss. The girl coos and looks into the cradle.

I stand next to her and ache to hold my child, something that I'll never be able to do again. I want to touch her, and I reach out. The girl brushes her cheek as if shooing away a fly.

She gently scoops up Molly and bounces her. "What a sweet baby." I can tell that Molly also likes her.

Mother Bradshaw runs a finger down the Molly's leg. "The dear thing is a trifle spoiled." She inflicts a small pinch and Molly yowls and the new Mrs. Bradshaw has a look of horror on her face. She has eyes to see them better than I did. She looks at Noel to gauge his reaction. She sees the sneer on his face. She looks back at Mother Bradshaw. "Where are the diapers? I think she needs a change."

Mother Bradshaw waves a disinterested arm in the general direction of the supplies.

The girl says, "Why don't I take care of this? I'm here now."

I feel the firmness of her voice. She's staking her territory.

Noel and his mother gladly agree and leave the room.

The girl gathers what she needs and lays Molly on a cloth on the dresser. She whispers, "Don't you worry, dear thing. I'm here now. I'll take care of you."

My heart leaps. I stand near her. "Thank you."

She stands up straight and looks about the room. She's shaken but does not run. She's made of stern stuff. She whispers, "Are you the mother?"

I say louder, "Yes."

She quickly changes the diaper and says, "I promise I'll take care of her and love her as my own. You should move along. And I can help you, if need be. My gran taught me about such things. She's helped many souls pass on."

In an instant all has changed. I see a future where my

daughter is happy and healthy. And a young, respected widow runs a prosperous ranch. I move closer to her. "But first you need to learn how to deal with snakes."

BETTINA AND FAYE SAVE THE DAY
BY VP CHANDLER

"Here it is on the right, Ivy Oaks. I've heard it's the swankiest, newest, most 'it' place to live now. I guess Sandra's husband's got a plush job."

"Faye, that's kind of rude."

"Well, we both know that her administrative assistant's salary sure ain't gonna pay for it."

"That's true. Still, rude."

"So, what'd you get her for the baby shower?"

"I picked something off her gift list. It'll be delivered in a couple of days. Today I'm bringing a card and a few jars of my famous chow chow."

"Ha! Me too. A gift card and some jars of homemade picante sauce. This batch is good, but the peppers were extra hot this year. Remind me to warn her about it."

"She's a Texas girl. She'll be fine. Oh! Is that the entrance up there?"

"Yeah. Turn in. Wow, this place has nice wide streets. Ka-ching."

"And all of the lawns are so green. I bet the HOA's a bear."

"Probably. Let's see, okay. GPS says to take a left on Oaklawn, go two streets and take a right on Ivy Lane, then we'll take a left on Oakdale."

"Oh, look at that nice old man watering his lawn. I've never understood why people stand there with a water hose. Seems inefficient to me. Use a sprinkler. But nice houses."

"Yeah, they're nice and all, and ...they look exactly the same. Even the colors. Bo-ring."

"You're right. I wonder why it's considered such a hot neighborhood?"

"Maybe the houses're really nice inside?"

"Faye, look at those kids riding bikes. How nice. Seems like you don't see that much these days. So, I guess there's a good side to this place too. Okay, I'm supposed to take a left on Oaklawn?"

"Yeah. Wow, look at all them turns on the GPS. What a maze. That's crazy."

"Wait, what happened to the GPS? Why is it blank now?"

"Probably just dropped cell service for a sec. I remember that you're supposed to take a right on Ivy Lane and then after a few streets, take a left on Oakdale. I don't recall the rest but maybe the GPS will kick in by then."

"Okay. Right here and then left on Ivy Lane. But this street has a different name."

"B, slow down. There's someone getting her mail. Maybe we could ask her? What the hell? Now why'd she run away like that?"

"Weird. Maybe she's just afraid of strangers."

"Probably afraid of anything that's different from the cookie cutter life. Maybe that's why she's living here. Look, there's another old man watering his lawn. Let's ask him."

"Faye, Is...is that the same old man?"

"Naw, the other one was wearing a yellow shirt."

"Okay, I'm confused. Let me stop for a second. Can you get GPS on your phone?"

"Nada. You?"

"Nothing. I swear that man has the same face as the first one we saw."

"You're weirding me out. He's wearing a different shirt, and he's on a different side of the street. It's a different man."

"Fine. I'm going to pull up. Roll down your window and ask him for directions."

"Howdy! Excuse me. Do you know how to get to 1221 Swedish Ivy Lane? Hello? Um, hello?"

"Faye, is he okay? Why is that man staring at us with his mouth open? Why is he...not moving at all? Oh my gosh. Is he having a stroke?"

"B, is his mouth buzzing? Do you hear that? It's like static."

"You're imagining things. You've seen too many creepy shows. Maybe it's from those huge power lines over there. They can make a humming noise. Let's keep driving."

"Okay. Damn, still no service. I can't believe this. So much for a 'desirable neighborhood'. And now we're gonna be late. Were there any directions on the invitation?"

"No. You know what, Faye? We've driven around for ten minutes and can't find any of the roads we're looking for. We're lost and this is too crazy. It's past noon now and it's baking hot, even with the AC on. Let's just go home. Sandra'll get her presents in the mail. We'll say we couldn't make it. Let me turn around."

"I agree. I could really go for a margarita right now."

"You're always in the mood for a margarita.."

"Look, there may still be hope. There's a lady that we could ask. Wait, doesn't she look almost exactly like that other lady who ran away from us?"

"Oh my god. She could be a clone of the other one. But she's wearing a flower print dress."

"B, stop the car. Red Oak Drive? I don't remember passing Red Oak Drive. Are we losing our minds?"

"No, let's keep going. I'm sure we'll recognize a street sign or something."

"Shit, B. We've been driving around for ten more minutes, and I think we're even more lost than before. Oh my GOD. Is that another old man like the other one we saw?"

"Can't be. This one's wearing a baseball cap. But what the hell? Is he not moving, either?"

"I tell you, we're in "Invasion of The Body Snatchers." I swear."

"Faye, you and your sci-fi imagination."

"Look, we need to start being smart about this. Something's wrong. I remember that the entrance to the subdivision is on the north side. It's past midday so if the sun is to our left or to our back, we'll be heading north. Let's try that."

"Okay. Sounds smart. Faye, there's a wall! We must be on the west side of the development! I bet Rockdale Avenue is just on the other side!"

"So close, yet so far. You know what? Pull over and I'll see if I can peek over the wall or get on it to see what direction we should go."

"Sounds good to me."

"Hello? Anybody on the other side of this wall? Hello? We need help!"

"Climb on top!"

"It's too tall. I'm getting back in the AC. I heard traffic and called out for help. No one. And that humming's gotten louder."

"Shit."

"Bettina! I think that's the first time I've ever heard you say a cuss word."

"I think it's deserved. I'm tired of this heat and roaming around. This is crazy."

"Agreed. I guess let's try to follow the wall north."

"Okay. We've followed the wall for several streets. I feel like we're making progress. So far so good. Oops. I lost sight of the wall. Do you see it? I'm concentrating on driving."

"I don't see it. Back up a little and we'll see where it is. Do you feel that? Is that the car or is the ground shaking?"

"Let me roll down my window. That droning is louder. I can't tell where it's coming from. Oh my god, Faye, Look behind us! There must be dozens of them! Are they replicas of the people we've seen over and over? Oh my god. They *are* replicas!"

"This is too crazy. It can't be happening."

"They're running at now! What is happening?"

"They're fast. Go! Go! B, get us outta here!"

"Too late, we're surrounded! What do we do?"

"Look for weapons?"

"We don't have any. All I see is your chow chow and my picante sauce. I can't think straight with them rocking the car. Hey! Get off my car! I just finished making payments on it!"

"Well, I ain't going down without a fight. If chow chow and picante sauce are our weapons, so be it. Maybe we can at least make their eyes burn. Let's pop these things open!"

"Okay. Done. Now what?"

"Fling it at them! Go for the face, their eyes and their open mouths. Open the doors on three—one. Two. Three! Take that, alien clones!"

"And that!"

"B, it's working! They're burning, like, melting! Maybe it's the vinegar in the sauce! Look! They're all turning around and running back to the noise."

"Thank god!"

"B, this is our chance."

"What do you mean?"

"This is our chance to get to the bottom of all of this."

"You've lost your mind. Let's go get help. Let's try to get away."

"And go where? We've got no GPS. Grab your last jar of sauce and follow me."

"Faye, I'm worried about you. Where are you running off to?"

"B, over here. Keep up."

"I'm trying. I'm not used to running at full speed and dodging behind bushes. And it's still hot as sin out here. Let's rest a second behind this bush. Hey, I didn't know you could run so fast. You work out?"

"Of course. A woman has to stay in shape these days. You never know what you'll face."

"Like alien clones taking over a neighborhood?"

"Exactly! Now look, they've all gone into that large building that looks like a community hall. Let's sneak up closer."

"Ugh. Of course."

"I see that they're getting washed off or something in a cave-like room. While they're busy, let's poke around and see who or what's in charge."

"Should we ask for a manager? I'm worried about you, Faye. You should be more scared. You almost seem like you're enjoying this."

"Whatever. You know, the way this place is organized, it reminds me of a beehive or an anthill."

"I want to leave."

"Think! This is science! I wonder if there's a queen."

"I just want to go home."

"Look, there's a green light coming from a room up ahead. Let's go check it out."

"Faye, slow down."

"Come take a look at this. See, I told you!"

"Everything about this is crazy. Oh my god. What's that thing? It looks like a giant larva that's laying eggs. Where's the top? Looks like she's so big that she goes up to another level above us."

"It's a queen and she's laying eggs! I bet they'll like pods for replicas. Just like in the movies!"

"I think I'm going to throw up. Really. I need to put my head down. Faye, is this real? Is this really happening? Please, I just want to go home."

"B, take a deep breath. I know this is crazy. I'm terrified too. But think about it. What can we do? We don't know how to get out of here. And those things won't let us. We have to be proactive to change our situation. Let's get close enough to see what our sauces do to her. Then you can throw up. Vomit has incredibly strong stomach acids. Why, that would likely do even more damage than picante sauce."

"Oh my god. More science?"

"More science."

"Faye, I feel sick, and you've gone insane. But I've never seen you more alive."

"Let's go. Don't trip over that green cable, or whatever that is. Ew, look at her. She's a great big worm with jagged teeth. Hey! You! Mama alien! You're messing with the wrong people! That's right! Haven't you heard of 'Don't mess with Texas?' Take that!"

"And that!"

"She's melting! It's working!"

"Yay! Is, is she supposed to melt that much? That's...getting gross."

"Um, yeah. That's a lot. It's like a chain reaction. Ew, now it's going up to the upper level. That's gonna make a big mess. It's raining green goo. Let's get outta here! Don't slip!"

"Oh my god, Faye, the smell. And so much of it. It's like a green rising tide! I'm going to puke."

"Follow me. Come on!"

"Faye, wait. Listen. The clones. They're wailing. Are you hearing that? Sounds like something's happening to them too!"

"Maybe, or they're mad. You know what? Let's end this once and for all. I bet they have a command center around here. Let's find it."

"The command center? We just killed the queen. Isn't that enough? Faye, this isn't Star Trek or Star Wars or whatever shows you watch."

"Yeah? Well, this sci-fi-loving hick woman is saving our hides. Over there, that looks promising. You know what? I bet our cellphones don't work because they're using something to jam the signal. If we can undo it, maybe we can get home. See, over there, control panels!"

"I hope so. I'm hanging on by a thread. Now, what the hell do all these symbols on these panels mean?"

"I've no idea. Just start pushing buttons and keep checking your cell phone to see if we can get a signal."

"That could take forever."

"Possibly."

"Faye, I'm tired and I think shock is setting in."

"I think I'm on to something. I think this sun symbol seems to mean on/off and this wavy sign I think means some kind of waves. Let me try to turn off the waves. Oh! The humming's dying! Check your phone!"

"Oh my god! I have a signal! Let's get out of here!"

"Maybe we should blow up the joint before we go."

"No! Let's go home and let someone else clean up the mess. The queen's gone. The clones aren't after us. *I need to get out of here, now.*"

"You're right. And I wouldn't want to be here if alien rein-forcements show up. Let's go. Let's start getting back to the car."

"Thank god for GPS. It'll be good to be heading home."

"And thank god for picante sauce and chow chow. Who would have thought that flinging it on aliens would melt them?"

"You know what, Faye? I don't think I'll ever make fun of you again for watching sci-fi movies and keeping up with science. I didn't know you were so into it."

"Thanks. I wanted to be a scientist or maybe even an astronaut when I was young, but people told me I'd make a good secretary instead. You know, women weren't supposed to be astronauts back then."

"No wonder you seemed like you were in your element. Those people were idiots. And you're amazing. Ah, home sweet car. Let's crank up the AC. Oh, that's wonderful. You know what? I'm feeling much better. And believe it or not, I'm now actually hungry. We've gone most of the day without eating. Let's go to Sammy's and eat some good Tex-Mex. I bet the sunset will be nice. And we can celebrate our escape and your triumph."

"Sounds good. But no guacamole. I've had enough green stuff for today."

"Ditto."

"B, do you know what I'm now wondering? Is Sandra one of them or one of us?"

"Oh, Faye. I hadn't thought of that."

"If she shows up at the office on Monday…"

"Let's have some chips and salsa in the break room. And then we'll see."

"And then we'll see."

"Who knows, Faye? Maybe your alien fighting days aren't over. Maybe you'll be the top alien fighter on our planet."

"You know what B? I could live with that. Now let's go get some frozen margaritas."

PART III

IF THERE BE NONE, NEVER MIND IT

F amily.

A WORD more loaded than a gun for some, a comfort of knowing for others. Family promises much but often falls short, even in the hands of those with the best of intentions.

WE ARE TIED BY BLOOD, by lore, by expectation, by pride. We attract and repel certain members of our clan, driven by our own desires to be seen and heard by those who share our ancestry.

WE RUN towards family and away from family, sometimes all in the same day.

. . .

BUT IN THE rubble of relationships often live the tiny diamonds of understanding, of shared appreciation, that can only be found if we're willing to dig deep and long enough. There is no guarantee those treasures will be unearthed, but we plow the ground with hope.

SOMETIMES WHEN WE DIG, we only fall deeper, lured by the child in us, hand outstretched, face towards the sun, waiting for guidance.

IT'S A GAMBLE, family.

Laura Oles

THE DEED

BY LAURA OLES

Previously published in *Denim, Diamonds and Death: Bouchercon Anthology 2019*

My first instinct as I stood in front of my childhood home was to burn it down.

I had been out of my car for a few minutes, and I could feel the sweat on my scalp beneath my ponytail. I reached up and wiped my brow with the back of my hand. The sun shone her spotlight in full force. No one should willingly visit South Texas in July. Like fried hell, a friend once told me. As much as I loved my home state, I despised the summers. They tested me in ways only another local would understand. Kingsville is a town of mixed fortunes, close to Corpus Christi and the Gulf Coast but also near the brutal brush lands of South Texas. Not blessed with island breezes but only steamy, rolling air disrupting dry grass and low bushes as it travels across the grounds. The town's claim to fame has always been the King Ranch. The King Ranch is low-key famous here. The enterprise—and it is an enterprise —covers more land than the entire state of Rhode Island.

Romantic visions of Santa Gertrudis cattle being rustled by

skilled vaqueros aside, my reality growing up here was quite different.

As wonderful as the Wild Horse Desert is for many, my favorite memory of the town was seeing it in my rearview mirror.

Yet here I was, back in the one place I vowed never to return. I remained a good distance from the house, the lot surviving solo on a vast field without another structure in sight. No cattle, few trees. Twenty acres of isolation. Just the way my father liked it.

It's lonely out here, I'd say to him.

I hated this house. And now it's the only thing of value I own.

I stared at the building, straining to summon even a single good memory. The house stood defiant, battered from years of neglect and the harsh glare of the land's relentless summers. It was a single-story ranch with weathered blue paint and traces of white trim. The right side of the stairs showcased a sagging wooden railing, large, jagged splinters dangling like icicle lights but without the festive sentiment. Remnants of a mesh screen whispered in the corners of the doorframe. The windows, hazy with an opaque grime, offered no hint as to what was inside. The roof drooped. The place was probably worth more flat.

I stared at the porch and thought of my mother. She spent much of her time there after her shifts at the Cypress Café. I would sit with her after she had finished mowing the front yard, so proud of that riding mower she'd bought at a town auction. Practically stole it, she boasted. As I entered my teenage years, almost a decade after she left, I often wondered if she missed that veranda more than she missed us.

The sound of a diesel truck interrupted my thoughts. The engine's violent rumbling demanded my attention long before the vehicle was close enough for me to recognize the driver. He thundered up the dusty road, raising high a trail of gritty debris. He parked behind my Tahoe, glancing at me but avoiding eye contact, before stubbing out his cigarette. Smoke separated around the door as he swung it open.

"Checking out your lottery ticket?" Carl's eyes found mine, the lines on his face deeper, more pronounced since I'd last seen him. Twenty years ago. Nicotine and the Texas sun had left their marks. His dark hair was longer now but the accusation in my big brother's eyes was just as I remembered. Some things never change.

"Funny. Somehow, I don't feel like a winner."

Carl turned his head and spit on the ground. "You know, he just gave this place to you because he was pissed at me."

"I can't imagine Jim being angry at you for anything, perfect son that you were." I kept his accusing stare and raised him some sarcasm. He didn't intimidate me anymore, not like when we'd been kids and he'd held our father's favor. He seemed smaller than I remembered, his stance more rounded, his ability to take up space reduced. Life had landed a few blows. I had the one thing he wanted, and we both knew it.

"So, what happened?"

"If I tell you, will you give me the deed?"

"Hell, no," I said, enjoying the rare experience of having the upper hand in our relationship. It was new territory, and I was a bit drunk from the rush. Was this what it had been like for him during our childhood?

"This place isn't worth much," I said. "I mean, it's not like we're in the middle of San Francisco. The house is probably a total demo, so it's down to the land." I signaled to the roof.

"Look at it. Bet it leaks inside."

Carl reached inside his shirt pocket and pulled out a pack of cigarettes. He held it out after pulling a single stick from the package. I shook my head, tempted, but refusing to fail in front of him. "I quit."

He shrugged and then smiled at me after lighting his Marlboro. Asshole.

"You going inside?"

"Not sure yet," I said, my eyes focused on the house. I didn't want to go in alone but I damned sure wasn't about to admit it. I didn't want to return to that loneliness. He and I both knew he could sense my fear.

"I'll go with you if you want." Bastard. "Wonder what it looks like now. It's been a while."

"When's the last time you were here?" I was curious now, about his relationship with our father and what had caused it to sour. Maybe letting him inside would loosen him up about the things I really wanted to know.

"Ten years. More, maybe." He pulled a long drag from his cigarette and stubbed it out with his Justins, the dust kicking up as he moved his foot from side to side. I envied him that moment. I missed smoking.

"Really? That long?" His answer surprised me. I had left this family behind as soon as I could hold down a full-time job and cover my own rent. In my mind, I had left them a tight unit, a family of two, the women long gone.

He extended his arm out to direct me ahead. I walked up the dusty path to the porch, careful with each step up as I made it to the front door. Carl waited for me to reach the top before putting any weight on the bottom stair. He didn't trust the structure, either.

I pulled the key from my pocket, two copies affixed to a simple metal ring with the address written on a paper tab. The lock refused to turn. I leaned in with a shove and played with the key.

After some jiggling, the lock gave way. I waited a beat, turned to look at Carl for I wasn't sure what—encouragement?—and pushed open the door.

The inside smelled of rot and neglect. A mixture of stale food and warm sour air filled the space. I swung the door open and closed to move some newer air through the place.

Then I went to a nearby window.

"Was he really living like this?" I asked as I struggled to unstick the window frame.

"I guess so. No family here to clean up except us, so..."

"I'm not cleaning this," I replied, perhaps with too much venom in my voice. "I did enough of that as a kid."

To say Jim had let the place go was like saying the Pope leaned towards religion. Still sparsely furnished, I stepped ahead into the living room, Carl following behind. Jim's favorite couch was flanked by yellowing stacks of newspapers, magazines, and other assorted papers. The wood paneling was in poor shape, chipped and sagging, and the other couches and chairs were ripped with stains across the dark green fabrics. All of it needed to be tossed out. I walked past the mess and checked out the kitchen. There was a stack of dishes and plastic cups piled in the sink, a few flies buzzing around, the only real sign of life. The beige counters were littered with items ranging from needle nose pliers and hammers to a box of random cables so old as to be considered useless. I decided against opening the fridge. No good could come of that.

I moved towards the dining room and saw that the space had been claimed for storing yet more useless crap. The wood table I remembered was still in the center, with two chairs on each side, the floral fabric faded from the sun streaming through one window. Piles of boxes filled with everything from crockpots to auto parts lined the walls. One thing in the room brought a small smile to my face.

"I remember when Dad let me pick out that wallpaper," I

said, pointing to the diamond patterned surface decorating the far wall. The stacks of boxes covered most of it now, and papers were piled so high that the pattern barely peeked from the corners.

Carl walked over to examine my childhood decision-making prowess.

"That was the summer I was at baseball camp," Carl said. "Got back and Mom was gone." I studied his face and realized how much our mother leaving had hurt him, too. Being six years older, he must have remembered more about her than I did, and growing up, I'd resented him for it.

"Yeah," I said, gesturing to the peeling paper, "I guess her leaving lit a fire under him. He decided we needed to redo the dining room. Had Larry over here helping him with some construction stuff, and he took me to Corpus to pick it out. Said I could choose whatever I wanted. Even stopped at Dairy Queen on the way home."

"Larry died a few years ago," Carl said. "Heart attack. Probably too much chicken fried steak. Heard about it when I was in town. He was really the only friend Dad still had."

I stood for a few moments, basking in the memory of that day. I didn't want to remember him fondly but maybe leaving me this house had involved more than simply spiting his son. Maybe it was his way of apologizing to me.

Carl walked through to the back bedrooms. I considered following him but let him be. I didn't want to go any further. If the living room and dining room were any indication, I'd seen enough. The place was a disaster. Now that I'd seen the inside, I knew the lot would be worth more without the house on it.

"Bedrooms are horrible, too," Carl said, returning from the back, his gaze moving from the kitchen to the living room and back again. "Couldn't get him to get rid of anything. We used to fight about it. All this worthless crap."

"On his way to full blown hoarding." I tried to reconcile what I observed with what I remembered growing up. Even after my mother had gone, the place had at least still been clean. I then realized it was because cleaning had become my job. There'd been no one to fill the position once I left.

"Didn't Jim have any other friends?" I asked.

"He hated that you called him that, you know." Carl's expression softened for the first time since he'd arrived. I tried to feel sympathy but couldn't muster it.

"He didn't act like a dad, so why would I call him that?" I could feel my jaw tightening and reminded myself to take a breath. "You were his favorite. I was the maid."

"I think you looked too much like Mom," Carl said, his candor surprising. "You really were the spitting image. Drove him nuts."

I shrugged. "Well, none of matters now."

Carl signaled to the front door. "C'mon, Nat, let's get out of here. How about we hit Cypress Café for dinner? Old times' sake?"

I nodded, following him out the door and closing it behind me. Maybe I should give him the house, I thought. Then I scolded myself for being too soft.

The Cypress Café had experienced a facelift since my last visit two decades ago. A wooden plaque with current typography and clean lines had replaced the faded metal sign I remembered.

Located between Herschel's Barber Shop and Henry's Pharmacy in a restored brick building downtown, the café was doing steady business as we approached the glass door. I wondered if there was anyone left that ever talked about my mom.

We walked in and the cold artificial air blasted us in the face. I welcomed it. We chose a booth towards the back.

"Can you imagine Mom working here?" I asked, once the waitress had left us to consider our order. I couldn't reconcile my memories of her and this place. "It's so different now. Nothing like I remember."

"The leftovers she'd bring home were my favorite dinners," Carl said.

I nodded. She always thought the cook had a thing for her. Just another rumor for the list."

"New owners took over six years ago," Carl said, looking over his shoulder to survey the restaurant. "I like it. Still a diner, but updated, you know?"

We sat making small talk until our food arrived. It was surprising how civil we could be over Cokes and barely shared memories. My BLT covered most of the plate, with a healthy serving of French fries threatening to spill over the side. Carl's chicken fried steak and mashed potatoes looked delicious but also reminded me of Larry and his heart attack.

"So," I said, between bites of my sandwich. "What happened?"

Carl shoveled a healthy portion of chicken fried steak in his mouth and chewed. He took his time before answering. "There was a period that I wanted to try to find Mom and we had some huge fights about it. He said she left us, and I didn't need to go looking for answers I'd never get.

I kept pushing him and finally he said he was going to give you the house just to piss me off." He took a sip from his water glass. "It worked." He shrugged. "Besides, Mom's parents died when she was little and she was an only child, so who was I going to ask?"

"Tell me what you heard about Mom leaving," I said. I looked down at my plate and played with the napkin in my lap, avoiding eye contact. "I was only eight, and all I heard were rumors and what Jim said."

Carl leaned back in his seat crossed his arms. "Why should I answer your questions now?

You took off and never looked back. You left me to handle Dad alone."

I'd gotten too comfortable with him, thinking our relationship may have healed a bit during this single day together. His comment was the match that lit my anger. I threw my napkin on the table. "You were always his favorite, Carl!" I glanced around and realized I had the attention of half the patrons in the place. I lowered my voice and leaned closer to the table. "Would you have stayed if he had treated you the way he treated me?"

"I know it was tough, but you did the same thing Mom did. She left and that was it. No looking back. She was gone, and then you were gone."

I pushed my plate to the side of the table. "Maybe Mom's leaving taught me that I could start over, too. Maybe she got tired of juggling an alcoholic husband and two kids. She got a fresh start, no matter how much it hurt us. I realized I could do the same thing. So I did. And I didn't owe Jim an explanation then, and I don't owe you one now."

I stood up to leave. It was foolish to think that the death of our father could tighten our bond. Carl looked up at me and gestured for me to sit back down. My first impulse was to leave, to berate myself for ever coming back here, let alone for agreeing to meet Carl at the house. But I returned to my seat and reached for my water glass. I could still feel dust in the back of my throat.

This town.

He said, "I don't know much more than you do. They were fighting a lot. Mom would come home after her shift here and give him a hard time about sitting on the couch and drinking beer all night. She wouldn't hand over her tips because he'd just spend it at the liquor store."

I remembered the arguing but not many of the details. I'd hide in my room. The walls were thin but at least the voices were muffled. Lots of yelling and breaking of dishes. I wondered if there were some things I didn't see, being young and avoiding their rows.

"There were rumors going around that she left to be with some other guy. Dad even said that, but I never believed him," Carl said, finishing the last of his steak. "Kids at school would say stuff sometimes, but you know, I tuned it out. Got used to acting like I didn't hear what they were saying."

"You were pretty lousy to me when I was a kid," I replied, my eyes now meeting his. "It was so hard without Mom there, and you and Dad were like buddies. I was alone."

Carl leaned in. "I know, Nat. I was fourteen. I took it out on you."

I reached toward him and tapped on the table.

"I have an idea and it's cheaper than therapy. You want in?"

Carl raised an eyebrow. "I'm listening."

The next day, I drove up to the house and found Carl had beaten me there. He stood leaning against his old diesel, smoking a cigarette, legs crossed, his boots making an X in the dirt.

"You got the tools?" I called from the window of my Tahoe. "I brought sledgehammers, gloves and some plastic bags."

Carl reached inside his truck and pulled out a metal toolbox. I recognized it immediately, and he took note. "He gave it to me a long time ago."

I nodded towards the house. "Not like he was fixing things around here anyway."

For the first time, I looked forward to going inside the house. It was time to put some ghosts to bed. For good. I refused to be haunted any longer.

"You sure about this?" Carl asked. "You won't change your mind later? Maybe the house is worth something still."

I shook my head, confident in my decision. "Even if it were, it would have to be brought to the studs." I carried my tools to the front door. "I'm sure. Let's do this."

Once inside, we made quick work of opening all the windows to circulate the stale air. Carl went back to his truck and returned with goggles and a box of trash bags. I handed him a set of work gloves, and we decided to split spaces. He would handle the kitchen because the cabinets were going to be tough. I chose the dining room. It seemed like the right place for me to start.

Carl swung his sledgehammer with force, making quick work of the kitchen counter. I moved an entire row of boxes to the side, clearing the way for my diamond-patterned wallpaper to be released from its misery. Sweat dripped off my brow and down my back, and I took a break to stick my head out an open window. The fresh air helped my resolve.

"Okay," I called. "Say goodbye to the dining room!"

I took the sledge over my head and swung it toward the wall. It was heavier than I expected, and I didn't do more than poke a neat little hole between two of the diamond shapes. Carl observed my novice technique and came over.

"Put it in your left hand first," he instructed, "and then swing it more like a baseball bat.

Maybe that would be easier for you."

I gestured toward the wall for him to take a swing, but he declined.

"Nope. This one is all you."

I nodded and took his advice, finding it easier to swing at an angle. I made contact with the wall and created a bigger hole. I thought of all the years of loneliness in the house, of being isolated and misunderstood. I swung again. A section of the wall pushed back, and I reached over and pulled the wallpaper and drywall towards me. I kept swinging, and the circle widened, a large section collapsing inward. I reached over to pull the piece out and stopped cold.

"What is that?" I asked Carl as I leaned in. White plastic peeked out from the hole I had created, but it was clear there was more hidden behind the wall.

"Workers leave trash all the time inside walls," Carl explained. "Old cans, papers, whatever."

He gestured for me to stand back. "Let me take a swing on this side."

He struck the surface with force and punched a new hole, pulling down and toward the floor with the hammer. An even bigger section of the came apart. Carl and I both dropped our tools and worked on pulling the ruined pieces back. Sections of the diamond-patterned paper scattered on the floor like leaves. With one more pull, I opened a large gap and found a piece of tan fabric.

I picked it up and immediately recognized it.

I held it in my hands, stretched out for Carl's examination.

An apron.

From the Cypress Café.

I held it, the wrinkled fabric of the front pockets showing a single piece of paper inside. I kept the apron in one hand and pulled out the paper with the other. I could never forget that handwriting.

I'm so sorry, Marie. I didn't mean it.

I looked at Carl as I considered what might be behind the wall. Heat enveloped me my heart beat loud in my ears, my face going flush. My legs gave way and I reached for Carl. He grabbed my arm and we hit the floor together. We hugged each other tight, the first time we'd done that since we'd been kids.

"Ms. Tillman?" Sheriff Martinez stood over me as I sat on the front porch, my head between my knees. Lightheadedness would come and go. I moved my head slowly upward, shading my eyes against the sun with my hand.

"Is it true?" I asked.

He scratched the top of his ear. An enormous Stetson covered his head. "We may need a DNA test to be sure, but we don't know who else it could be in there." He knelt down next to me and placed his hand on my shoulder gently. "I'm really sorry you had to come back to find... this."

I waved my hand upward and returned my head to my knees to catch my breath. "Is Carl still inside?"

"Yes," he replied. "Should I send him out?"

I nodded and Sheriff Martinez went inside. Carl came and sat down and put his arm around me. I tucked the apron on the floor between my legs, unwilling to relinquish it just yet, even though the crime scene tech had asked for it a half hour ago. I had something of my mother's and I refused to let it go.

"I don't understand." I wiped my hair off my forehead, sticky from sweat, and used my shirt to dab the salt from my eye. "How could he?"

Carl put his hand to his lips. "I don't know, Nat. Things got pretty heated sometimes but I can't believe he'd..." He left the sentence unfinished, and I couldn't do it for him.

"All those years we'd thought she left us, and she's been right here." The idea that my mother's body had remained hidden behind the wallpaper I had chosen as a child turned my stomach. I took long breaths to slow the spinning of my world.

"She didn't leave us, Nat," Carl said, offering comfort.

I hugged him tighter. "Now I wish she had."

Carl and I moved away from the house and stood by his truck as Sheriff Martinez and the other officers continued their work inside. Numbness had taken over. I wondered what my dad's intention had been when he'd left me the house instead of Carl. He'd been trying to tell me something.

I knew I would never again step inside that place.

Sheriff Martinez came down the stairs towards us. "We'd like to take your statement soon if you're feeling up to it."

I nodded. "I think I can do that." I glanced at Carl. He remained leaning on his truck, smoking a cigarette, watching the activity coming in and out of the house.

"Let me know if there's anything I can do for either of you."

"Maybe there is," I said. I looked to Carl to get his attention. "Do you think the fire department would want the house?"

"For what?" the sheriff asked as he looked at Carl with an *Is she doing okay?* look in his eyes. "They can burn it to the ground if they want," I told him. "For practice. I hear they do that sometimes. We were going to demo it anyway."

"When we're done here, if you still want to donate it, I'll let them know."

"I'm sure," I said. "If you don't do it, we will."

Carl nodded in agreement. "She's right. The house can't stay standing."

The sheriff went back to his men, leaving Carl and I to stand on the sidelines. I had no idea what to do now. Everything I thought I knew was wrong.

I rested my head on my big brother's shoulder and cried.

24 HOURS IN SHINJUKU

BY LAURA OLES

Kate Walsh checked the hotel clock on the nightstand. A shade past four in the afternoon. Janine, her boss, and the rest of their team would soon be boarding their flight out of Narita. Four o'clock in Tokyo meant one in the morning back home in Austin. Plenty of time to fire off a revision to her colleague and have it waiting in his inbox before the office opened.

Her eyes settled on the black hard-shell case entrusted to her care. She had tucked it inside the small closet, nestled next to a safe the size of a large shoebox. She pulled the case towards her and rested it on her bed's white duvet. She released the latches. In the center of its custom foam-packed interior rested a VR headset prototype, a new product that would propel her employer far ahead of their competition. She double checked the contents one last time before closing the case and returning it to her closet, pulling a blanket from the top shelf and wrapping it over the case as some imaginary additional protection.

She scanned her hotel room. Her suitcase rested atop the brass stand, her clothes neatly organized inside it and her travel outfit folded over a nearby chair. Everything in place. A finely tuned machine, her ex had once remarked while traveling with her. She didn't believe he intended it to be a compliment.

Kate returned to the closet and adjusted the blanket before closing the door.

One more day and then she'd be on her way home.

Kate stood in the center of the Keio Plaza hotel lobby, scrolling through text messages on her phone. She glanced at her boots against the polished marble floor dotted with dark diamond shapes inlaid in repeatable pattern. The area harkened to the opulence of an older time, its majestic crystal chandeliers over-looking the sea of guests traveling through the space. Two tables hosted matching grand floral arrangements in various shades of cream and pink. The faint waft of lilies tickled Kate's nose.

She had spent the morning wandering the nearby area around Shinjuku station. She even managed to find her way to the Kinokuniya bookstore while using Google maps in kana and meters, then popped into a few shops on her way back to Keio Plaza. She feared straying too far from the areas she knew.

Now a shade past six o'clock and back in the hotel lobby, a throng of travelers eddied around her. A gentleman moving past her, his sleeve grazing her arm. His navy suit and white collared shirt blended in with the other travelers in his orbit. Her eye fell on the small enamel pin on his lapel. A white owl.

"*Gomen nasai*," he said as he straightened his rolling suitcase behind him.

"*Daijoubu desu*," Katherine replied with a smile and a slight bow. She hoped her limited Japanese properly conveyed that there was, in fact, no problem. She watched him as he navigated through the crowd until he reached the end of the hospitality counter line.

The pit in her stomach warned her that maybe this dinner meeting was a bad idea. She hadn't seen Jonathan in a year, and she knew as soon as she'd posted about a free night in Tokyo that he would reach out to her. She checked her phone again, scanning her messages to determine which required her immediate attention and which could be ignored until morning. Her phone vibrated.

Walking towards front entrance.

The sliding doors of the Keio Plaza hotel remained in a constant state of flux. January was appropriately brisk, and Katherine had taken to always keeping a scarf and gloves on her.

She watched him enter the lobby, a few pounds lighter than their last encounter. His charcoal jacket peeked open, revealing an olive and navy scarf. A birthday gift she'd given him years ago. Things were different between them then.

Jonathan smiled, his eyes on her as he weaved through a crowd of twenty-somethings dressed for a night out. He extended his arms, hugging her as though they were long lost friends, not former colleagues and briefly lovers who had parted ways after failing to mix business with pleasure. His cologne still smelled of sage and cedarwood. They often joked that his scent lingered in the conference room long after he left. Before he'd left for good.

"Kate, you look amazing," Jonathan said, giving her a quick squeeze before releasing her from his grasp. "I wasn't sure that you'd agree to see me since my texts have gone unanswered."

Kate slipped her phone in her jacket pocket as if to hide the offending party. "I just needed some time to process the way you left." She had more to say, but it could wait. "It's nice to see you again," she said instead. And meant it.

"I know, I owe you apologies for a lot of things." He held his arm out. "Shall we?"

Kate looped her arm through his and followed his lead out of the lobby.

She stayed close to him as they walked down Fureai-Dori Avenue. Brisk winds whipped her dark hair around her face and into her eyes. She released her hand from Jonathan's arm to tuck it behind her ear. She continued walking next to him but disconnected now—if he noticed this tiny separation, he made no mention of it. Tokyo's pace required a quick step, the group ahead of them increased their distance at a noticeable clip.

The street greeted them with bright screens advertising JVC and other electronic brands, colorful neon signs, one highlighting a cat holding a microphone. Jonathan noticed Kate's prolonged gaze.

"Great karaoke place," he explained. I've taken a few friends there. Maybe we can go later if you're interested."

Kate shook her head. "Karaoke is strictly a spectator sport for me," she said.

"Can't carry a tune in a bucket?"

Ah, his love for cliches remained.

"Like cats brawling in a back alley."

Jonathan gestured towards the festival of neon signs enveloping them.

"There's simply no other place in the world like Tokyo," Jonathan said. "I've been here for six months now, and I'll hate to leave when my assignment's over."

The city's chaotic beauty wrapped around Kate, consuming her senses like a technicolor disco ball. She glanced at Jonathan, wondering if he mistook her satisfaction in the setting for her satisfaction with his company.

Kate followed Jonathan as he turned the corner. A small

yellow lantern decorated in kanji script stood at the corner of a simple door. Jonathan reached for the door and ushered her inside, following behind. The interior glowed in warm light. Several shades of polished wood decorated dining tables and booths. A bar dotted with patrons enjoying drinks at the opposite end of the restaurant. A young woman stood behind a hostess podium.

"*Konbanwa*," she said.

"*Konbanwa*." Jonathan gestured towards Kate and held up two fingers. "*Futari, desu.*"

The hostess nodded and gestured towards the floor. They would need to remove their shoes before dining. After Kate's first night fiasco of wearing ballet flats over bare feet with only an overdue pedicure peeking below her trousers, she added socks to her daily attire. After placing their shoes in nearby lockers, they followed the hostess to their table. Kate placed her small handbag inside the rectangular bin by her stool.

Once seated, Jonathan tapped his fingers on the table. "I can't believe it's been a year," he said.

He smiled but said nothing further on the topic. A waiter arrived with a glass carafe of water and two small glasses. Kate noticed a group of four diners occupying a nearby booth. One woman wore a stunning deep ruby jacket tailored with an intricate diamond brocade. She emulated art in motion.

Jonathan said, "I think we've shared enough dinners together that I can choose some things to your liking?"

"Of course."

Jonathan spoke to the waiter, pointing to several items on the menu. Once he'd departed, Jonathan said, "I take it you've enjoyed your time here?"

Kate clasped her hands together. "Definitely fallen in love with Tokyo. I'm going to miss the restaurants, the energy of the city, and the trains the most."

Jonathan reached for the carafe and poured water for them both. The waiter returned with two Kirin bottles and tall glasses.

"Do you miss Austin?" Kate asked, watching Jonathan reach over to pour the amber liquid into her glass before filling his own.

"I do, but being out of the country has been good for me," Jonathan said. "Everything was such a mess, and we couldn't both stay there." He sipped the foam from the top of his glass. "I'd been warned we weren't compatible, but you know, I thought our arguments added fire to our relationship."

"Fire is useful until you burn down your house with it," Kate replied.

"We really did torch all of it, didn't we?"

Kate tilted her head slightly. "We? I think you were the one with the match in your hand." She reached for her beer glass. "I'd been warned about you, but I guess I needed to learn who you really were on my own." All the anger she thought she'd laid to rest resurfaced in her words.

His smile abandoned his face, a touch of sadness now in his eyes. She only felt half guilty for the jab. After what he'd done, he deserved it.

"For what it's worth, I really cared about you."

"You should treat people you care about better," she replied. "Not just me. Our whole team. We were building something special."

Jonathan continued to sip his beer as Kate surveyed the restaurant. He then said, "I guess we should address the other elephant in the room."

"Well, he does seem to take up a lot of space."

He studied the beer bottle on the table for several moment before meeting her gaze. "I know you're mad at me for leaving Quantum Leap, but you also know I did everything by the book." Jonathan hid behind his beer.

"If you mean not technically violating your non-compete, that's true, but only because you found a loophole by being hired by another subsidiary. I'm pretty sure Janine still has a voodoo doll in her office with your name on it. She received plenty of push pins as gifts from the staff you left behind."

Jonathan shook his head. "Wow. First of all, I loved our team. You know that. I spent five years with QL, but I also thought we weren't executing fast enough." It was a common complaint, not only at QL but in many other tech-focused companies, too. Silicon Valley's motto of "move fast and break things" had come at a cost, and the industry now had to grapple with the ethical and human costs of progress at any price.

"Janine knows what you did before you left."

The waiter arrived with appetizers, giving Jonathan a brief reprieve. "This looks amazing," Jonathan. A selection of gyoza, chicken katsu and edamame in small ceramic bowls covered the table's surface. She lifted her chopsticks and reached for a dumpling, dipping it in a tiny bowl of soy sauce. Jonathan busied himself rearranging some of the plates.

"You still want to play dumb?" Kate asked. "Fine." She placed her chopsticks on the small ceramic holder. "Janine knows you took your client list with you."

"They were my clients," Jonathan said in defense. He refused eye contact, his attention instead shifted to refilling his water glass.

"They were property of Quantum Leap, who paid for their development and outreach. You were the face of the company for them, nothing more."

"*If* I did such a thing," he said, reaching for an edamame pod, "I would have only taken those clients that threatened to jump ship, anyway." He tossed the empty pod into the disposal bowl.

"I guess if you can sleep at night..."

"I sleep great," he countered.

She believed him. She'd worked with him long enough to recognize that look. Whatever he'd done, he felt it was the right thing. His confidence was one of the things that drew her to him. He was right even when he wasn't.

"Regardless," she said, reaching for her Kirin, "I think you could have left under better circumstances."

He held her stare for the first time all evening. "You're right. I was angry when I left. You and I were over, and the team took your side. I was vilified for pushing for progress. And when Wired World came calling and offered me all I wanted and then some, I jumped at it. I have a feeling you might have done the same thing if the tables were turned."

"Maybe," Kate admitted. Being a woman in tech meant walking a fine line— strong but not domineering, over-preparing for the simplest meetings to be taken seriously. *Embrace being underestimated*, Janine had told her. Janine's advice had proven true in multiple situations. Kate could guide many aspects of development if the cocksure men on her team believed they were the ones in charge—and claiming credit.

"I hear you're doing cool things with LivingGlass," he said. "I don't think we'll be going into the VR space in that way. Just not enough money and adoption traction to make it work for us."

Kate claimed the last gyoza with her chopsticks. "It's a fascinating space. The demos we did here were very promising." She finished her beer and then said, "Of course, being in charge of the prototype makes me nervous. Janine couldn't take it with her due to luggage requirements, and no way she was going to check it."

Jonathan nodded. "That does sounds stressful." He pulled his phone from his pocket. "Sorry—one of my directors keeps asking for an update. Why he can't wait until the morning, I don't know." Their waiter arrived with the next round of offerings—salmon kushiyaki, yakatori negima and steamed baby bok choi—and Kate nodded her appreciation to their waiter while Jonathan finished his text.

"Janine knows you've been asking about LivingGlass, trying to get information."

Jonathan's expression offered mock offense. He placed his phone face down on the table. "Even if I did, no one was interested." He added, "All's well that ends well."

His love of cliches again. Kate reached for the baby bok choi first. "Enough sparring. Let's enjoy this gorgeous dinner."

"*Arigatō*."

Once dinner was done, Jonathan said, "I've got one more place I'd like to take you before you turn in for the night."

Kate hedged. "I don't know that I should stay out too late. Still have a lot of emails to handle."

"Don't waste your last night in Tokyo in your hotel room on your laptop." He shuddered. "I promise you'll have a good time." He flashed his megawatt smile. She'd fallen for it too many times.

"No karaoke, right?"

"Promise."

"Ok, but only for a bit," Kate protested. "I have to be up early."

He offered his hand. "Trust me."

As they stepped out into the brisk evening, Kate realized she was now dependent on Jonathan. She knew very little about Tokyo outside of the last few days she'd spent here, and while she could probably get home in a pinch, the busy streets with their winding curves, the disorienting bright lights and cold air reminded her that she was largely unfamiliar with her surroundings."

"So, where are you taking me?" Kate asked. She stared at a large neon sign showcasing attractive young women holding cameras and posing for one another.

"To a favorite small hangout I found through some friends," he explained. He pointed to the sign that had captured Kate's attention. "I wish we had time to visit some of these shops," he said. "I think you'd love Yodobashi and Bic Camera. Could easily spend an entire day in there."

"I've been told to stop at Don Quijote for my duty-free gifts."

He grinned like a child with a new toy. "You're going to lose your mind in there. Block at least an hour. It's crazy busy and so much to see."

Kate stayed close to Jonathan as they navigated through a group of teenagers bunched together in conversation. "It's just a little further," he said. Before long, they came upon an alleyway which led to a building. Kate looked up at the nondescript building, the exterior giving her no clues as to its purpose or occupants. He held the door open for her, and once inside, they walked a few short steps to the elevator.

"This area is Kabukicho," he explained. "My colleagues say it was once a red-light district, and it's got some fantastic bars and restaurants now." He pointed to the building above them. "This place is my new favorite haunt."

The elevator door opened, and Jonathan signaled to Kate to step inside. He pressed the top button. The doors opened and revealed a nondescript room with only a small black couch and an end table. An ash tray with a few scattered business cards nestled in the center were the sole decor. Bare walls. A black door faced them on the other side. "This way," he said. Kate followed him through the door and gasped once inside.

She had stepped back in time to a breathtaking speakeasy. A

cozy space, room for maybe a dozen people at the bar and a few two-top tables on the far end of the room. A large mirror covered the entire back wall behind the bar, and ornate bottles lined the full expanse from one end to the other A bartender poured bourbon over a large square ice cube in a short glass. "*Konbanwa*," she said as she addressed the pair.

"*Konbanwa*," Jonathan replied. "Muri, this is my friend Kate."

"So nice to meet you, Kate."

"Lovely to meet you as well."

She gestured towards two open spaces in the middle of the bar. Jonathan pulled the stool out for Kate, and she slid in, hanging her bag on the back of the chair.

"Two old fashioneds?" Jonathan asked. Kate nodded, and Muri reached for two glasses then pulled a knife from below the bar. She held a rough block of ice and chopped at it until she fashioned an ice globe with prism edges, her fingers nimbly turning it in small increments. The woman worked expertly, creating the same globe for the second glass before dropping it into a highball glass.

"This is the entire reason I order this drink," he explained. "Watching Muri work is the best part of this place. She's also the owner of Top Shelf."

"You're very kind," she said. She finished preparing the drinks and added a kumquat garnish before placing them on coasters. "Enjoy."

"*Kanpai*," Jonathan said.

"*Kanpai*." Kate held her glass up and touched his, the clank of the union louder than expected.

For a few moments, Kate allowed herself to enjoy the comfort of Top Shelf. Two women, both mid-twenties, commiserated over chardonnay. Three men in suits squeezed around a two top.

"So, is this better than being in your hotel room basking in the glow of your laptop?" Jonathan smiled as he held up his drink, the large, beveled sphere catching the light from above.

"I admit, I'm impressed." Kate felt the warmth of the liquor as she listened to Muri share her experiences of opening Top Shelf. Jonathan leaned in closer, and for just a moment, she allowed herself to fully enjoy his company. She missed this connection, his energy, his attention. She also knew the withdrawal wasn't worth the addiction.

Kate checked the time. "I can't believe it's already eleven. I should probably go soon."

"You'll be fine," he said. "You always get there early anyway."

"Military upbringing. What can I say?" Kate waved off a third drink. She leaned in closer to her former colleague. "You should know that Janine wouldn't be happy if she knew I had dinner with you tonight."

"What she doesn't know won't hurt her," he replied. "All is fair in love and war, right?"

There it was. That million-dollar smile.

That same smile shook her to her senses. She thanked Muri for her hospitality and then said to Jonathan, "I'd better get back."

"As you wish."

Kate sighed as she stepped into the Keio Plaza lobby. Jonathan's energy often invigorated and then drained her. Now alone, the adrenaline in her body had been replaced with fatigue. She'd been on guard the entire evening, and she was ready to lay down her sword. Kate navigated through groups of people, some returning from dinner and others preparing to leave for a night out. A man stood at the concierge desk talking with a woman in a black coat. Another couple seemed to quietly argue in a corner next to an art display.

Kate pulled her key card from her handbag. Once inside her room, she took a quick inventory. Nothing seemed out of place, although housekeeping had come in and turned down her bed for the evening, leaving a tiny white box with a single truffle in front of the pillow. She'd enjoy that chocolate once she'd had a proper shower.

Kate shed her coat and placed it on a nearby chair. She stood in front of the window, taking in Tokyo's impressive nightline. She'd miss this place. But she also missed home. Tokyo belonged to Jonathan now.

She turned to the closet. The door was closed as she'd left it. When she pulled the latch, she glanced and saw the blanket still covering the black hard-shell case. She bent over, cast the blanket aside and placed the case on the bed. She hesitated before opening the latches.

Click. Click.

She lifted the lid and stared at the interior foam padding. The center mold was empty. The LivingGlass prototype was gone. She reached for the blanket on the floor, and a small white glint caught her eye. She reached to the floor and picked up an enamel pin.

The snow owl.

The flight attendant stood at the entry of the aircraft as Kate stepped off the jet bridge and into the cabin. "Welcome aboard. Boarding pass, please?"

Kate held up her phone and was directed to her Business First seat. She offered her thanks and then placed her rolling bag in the overhead compartment. She removed the pillow and travel kit from her chair and placed it on the side wall of her pod. After sliding her messenger bag in front of her, she sat down and admired her surroundings. She normally occupied the economy plus seating. She far preferred this arrangement.

Kate pulled her phone from her bag and checked her messages. The flight attendant brought a glass of pinot noir and placed it on her table.

Janine: *All boarded?*

Kate: *Yes, love BF. Thank you.*

Janine: *Of course.*

Kate: *Everything working?*

Janine: *Confirmed. We're already receiving AV feeds from the headset.*

Kate: *Anything interesting?*

Janine: *Jonathan doesn't think much of either of us.*

Kate: *To his detriment*

Janine: *Agreed. Safe travels.*

She slipped her phone back in her pocket and turned her attention to the pinot noir. Her shoulders relaxed. The hard part was over.

Janine was right. Being underestimated was a competitive advantage.

Jonathan had taken the prototype because she'd let him. He would later learn—hopefully much later—that the VR goggles weren't so much a window into Quantum Leap's technology as it was their window into Jonathan's new employers. She thought of his tired cliches and offered one of her own.

Be careful what you wish for.

THE NIGHT SHIFT

BY LAURA OLES

Rae Ronson arrived home at seven in the morning to find her snoring sister face down on the living room couch, her sequin-laden uniform throwing light pattens against the wall. The sunlight streaming through the window created a disco-ball effect in the room. Light blue squares danced around the space. She had created Studio 54 with her backside. Dana snored loudly as Rae stood over her, taking in the sight.

Something had to change.

Las Vegas, with its flashy Strip and the promise of easy money cocktailing at casinos, had taken a toll on the Ronson sisters. Rae wondered how she'd ever come to this point, dragging her younger sister from one city to another, only to take yet another mediocre job that offered laughable wages in return. Rae had crossed the threshold into her thirties two years back with Dana's toe dangling on the same decade line. Dana had always looked to Rae for guidance but scanning her little sister's limp body sprawled across the brown sofa, Rae wondered if she really should have accepted the responsibility. She certainly didn't feel worthy of it. It was clear neither of them had a plan for a life outside of working for an hourly wage in form-fitting uniforms that teetered on the edge of trading dignity for dollars.

Rae reached over and shook Dana by the shoulder. "D, you know better than to fall asleep on the couch in that thing. The sequins are going to pop off and you won't pass inspection." She sighed. "And you know how expensive repairs can be. You don't want to be in the hole to the house."

Dana, still face down, reached a hand in the air towards her sister's voice. "I know. I know," she replied, her voice muffled by cushions. She moved her arms under her body and pushed herself up before rolling onto her side, taking note of the fringe, now wrinkled from her weight. She sat up on the couch and rubbed at her eyes. Her black eyeliner smudged towards her temple, the careful blue makeup now a mess of turquoise and glitter.

"I thought you were working until seven?"

Dana shook her head. "Was supposed to, but I only clocked four hours and they cut me loose. I had a chance to pick up Lottie's shift, so I thought I'd come home for a bit..." She leaned forward and picked up her cell phone from the coffee table, checked the screen and then placed it next to her on the couch. "I just didn't want to take all this off if I had to turn around and go back."

Rae nodded. Even the least ornate uniforms were still a hassle to put on and take off. Always a bit too snug in all the wrong places with shiny bits snagging every surface. She held her hand out to Dana, who took it, using it as leverage off the couch.

"We're getting too old for this," Rae said, her eyes trained on her sister's grimace as she rubbed her lower back.

"Speak for yourself. I'm still in my twenties."

"For another three months."

Dana cocked her head to one side. "I always thought I'd be doing something more important by now."

"Me, too." She reached for Dana and rubbed a smudge of eyeliner off. "I'm sorry I'm such a lousy career counselor," Rae replied.

"You made sure I got through high school," Dana said. "No way I would have done that unless you were on me all the time."

"I just wish I could have afforded to pay for college."

"Rae, you're the smarter one. If anyone should have gone to college, it's you."

Rae wasn't so sure. Growing up, their family life involved rummaging through the kitchen for food and hiding from their mother and her angry outbursts. Their dad had popped in and out of their lives between illicit jobs and state pen stays. Rae was sure he'd gotten the best deal out of all of them. She hated him for it. And she hated herself for being unable to forge a better life for her and her little sister. Dana was smarter than she gave herself credit for. She just lacked the confidence to follow through on things. Rae had to whisper in her ear, push her in even the smallest ways.

Reality's bright light blinded her like the sun streaming through her car's windshield during her afternoon commute.

As Rae glanced around their spare apartment, she knew it was time to move on. Two sisters slinging drinks in Vegas would not make a career. Working nights and sleeping days had been hard on Rae's body and even harder on her soul, and looking at Dana, she knew the path they were on led only to more of the same work for shit pay. Days had turned to weeks, and those weeks had become months and then years. They had little to show for it other than a roof over their head and stale leftovers in the fridge, which was certainly more than others in the city could claim.

It was time to move on.

It was time to plant roots.

It was time to build a life.

She pulled the bobby pins from her updo, remnant hair-spray keeping the strands fixed in place. Rae grimaced as she ran her hands through one side. She needed a shower and a good day's sleep.

But first, Rae took her phone out of her bag and sent a text to the one person she had vowed to never let back in her life. She wouldn't tell Dana. Not yet. Not until she had a plan to pull them out of his hole. She knew her sister would be angry with her for breaking their shared rule.

Never contact Victor.

Rae shuddered as she stood in front of the lobby entrance of the Ez Stay Motel. She scratched at her right arm, wondering if she was allergic to the place. Or allergic to who was behind the door. She couldn't shake the feeling that she was being tailed. Maybe it was because stepping into this world meant awakening old ghosts.

Victor's office was in Room 1313, on the first floor of the back building facing a side road that no sane person would venture on past sundown. Even daytime could be a hit or miss proposition. She stood as if her boots were made of lead, second guessing both the call she'd made and the lie she'd told to her little sister about checking out a job opportunity. She knew that if she knocked on his door, there'd be no going back.

She had no choice.

Victor considered himself a businessman, a staffing agency for those who needed a quick payday in dire circumstances. Nothing about Victor was legitimate, beginning with almost every decision he'd made since he was old enough to drive. Rae was certain that toddler Victor picked fights from his crib. But if you needed a payday off the books and didn't mind being leered at by random bad players, no one ran the quick job racket like Victor. His pockets were lined with his clients' desperation.

Victor also pulled some big jobs, but the last one landed him a nickel in lockup. Since then, he'd been more cautious about doling those out. But then again, the payday was sometimes worth the risk.

Rae walked to Room 1313, knocked on the door in the signature pattern and waited. A few moments later, the door opened.

"Nice to see you, Rae," Victor said, "You look like shit."

"Thanks," she replied. "And same."

Victor smiled at her, opened the door wider and gestured her inside. She peeked over his shoulder. No one else inside. She hesitated.

"He's not here." He ran his hand through his thinning brown hair. "Still shows up sometimes. Still asks about you."

Rae's shoulders remained tense. Wiley's presence still followed her, taking up valuable headspace, keeping her fight or flight instincts primed. She stepped inside and surveyed the grim surroundings that served as Victor's headquarters. Two large pizza boxes teetered dangerously close to the edge of the coffee table they rested on, and a scattering of empty beer cans gathered on the battered carpet. Rae nodded at the mess.

"Business dinner?"

"Something like that." He studied her as she studied the dim hotel room. "I thought you said I was dead to you."

"You still are," she replied. "But I need to pick up one last job." She glanced at the small couch in the corner and considered its surface before sitting down. "I need to get Dana out of this town. She deserves better."

He pulled a cigarette from a pack on his desk and grabbed a red plastic lighter. "Does she know you're here?"

Rae met his comment with silence.

"So, you looking for the same kind of work?" He walked over a small desk and checked his laptop. "I have a job you might like."

"Just something I can do without Dana finding out."

He continued to peck at his laptop. "This job's one you can do solo. No crew, pay comes to you directly once I get mine."

Rae's shoulders released at the idea of working alone. "As long as Wiley isn't involved."

"He really has a thing for you. Even after what you did to him."

"He started it. I just finished it."

Victor pulled a long drag from his cigarette. "Well, I'm pretty sure he still thinks he has some unfinished business with you."

Victor's comment landed cold. Her gut told her this was a bad idea, that she had other options. But did she? Her skills were valuable in limited circles, but they weren't resume-appropriate. She wanted a legitimate life, one that Wiley had called 'tiny and uninteresting.' He said she'd be bored with that soon, and she wanted to prove him wrong. More than anything, she wanted to prove to herself that she wanted those things. Her brief year with him had shattered her confidence in a thousand tiny ways. He was the reason she kept a knife in her bag and a gun in her car.

"You sure you want to do this?" Victor asked, noticing her thousand-yard stare. He almost sounded like he cared.

Rae choked down her doubt. "I'm sure."

Victor reached for a nearby notepad on his desk, the top page stained with coffee on the corner. She watched as he wrote a few lines, ripped the page, folded the paper, and handed it to her. He then pulled his desk drawer open and reached inside.

"You know the drill," he said, handing her the burner phone. "This one's going to turn soon, so keep your eyes on it."

Rae nodded and slipped her phone in her pocket. Her mind turned to how she would keep Dana in the dark—it would be easier this time, since her sister trusted her again. She hated that she was about to take a hammer to their newly rebuilt bond. She had no choice. She'd make Dana see it.

"Tell me about the job." Rae pushed a stack of napkins off a nearby chair and sat down. "What's so interesting about it?"

Victor's eyes brightened at the question. "It's a good one. Pay is above average because it's a sentimental item." He held his hand up, smoke wafting from the cigarette between his fingers. "A well-connected woman trusted the wrong man, who stole a very valuable piece of jewelry for collateral in a private poker game, then lost it by overplaying his hand. Turns out her mom was a high-profile mistress of a big boss back in the sixties and that's the only piece she had left. Sold everything else to pay the bills once she was replaced with a younger wife."

Rae didn't want to admit it, but Victor had hooked her with the story. And he was right that personal jobs often paid more than standard lifts—betrayal fuels the kind of rage that pushes prices higher.

"So, this woman is good for it? Money wise?"

Victor stubbed out his cigarette. "Oh yeah. Best part is the dude who won it has no idea about its heritage, at least from what I know. It's just another score from another game, but he knows he can't pawn it local. He uses a specialty guy for these kinds of wins, and Wallace doesn't come into town until Friday. So, we've got a little time, but not much."

Two days.

"You got a tail on this guy?"

"Yeah, I've got someone." He reached for another smoke and noticed Rae's clenched jaw. "He's solid."

She nodded. "So, his place doesn't have any cameras set up?"

"No way." Victor put his cigarette down in the ashtray. "His apartment's full of stolen stuff. He's not going to put that shit on the cloud."

"So, no roommates? Girlfriends? Alarms?"

"No, not anymore. He doesn't even sleep there most of the time. His brother has a house, crashes there. This apartment is just for inventory and meetings. Dude smokes a lot of pot, a little sloppy. He's lazy but he's good at cards and fencing."

"Why are you giving me this job?" Rae asked.

He shrugged his shoulders. "You asked for help. I always help you."

"I mean...why are you giving me this particular job?"

"It's pretty low risk with a high reward. And if you want to get Dana out of here and start over somewhere else, this job pays enough that it'll give you a solid runway."

"So, you trust me?"

"More than you trust me."

Fair.

Rae turned to leave the room. She glanced over her shoulder.

Victor winked. "Just like old times."

She hoped not.

Dana stood in front of the mirror, tugging at her bodysuit, her mouth tight. "I think I'm allergic to sequins now," she said. "I dream of the day when I have a job that doesn't require wearing this bullshit." Another tug at the suit, and a flat turquoise bead popped off in response.

"No one will notice," Rae said. She handed Dana her jacket. "You don't want to be late. Denny is a real jerk about that, especially since we're shorthanded."

The casino had lost several employees this month. The gig

had a regular turnover of talent. It was built into the business. Tips were down; some waitresses bounced for better hours or better pay, some left the hustle altogether for a new relationship or to work daylight hours. Nights were hard on the body and harder on the soul. Rae knew the only reason she and Dana had lasted this long was because they had each other and had built a clientele of regulars who sought them out and tipped well. Some held onto the hope that their financial attention would buy them more than a thank you, and the Ronson sisters walked a careful line. A customer could turn in a hurry. It had happened last year to Annie Vetters, but the casino covered it up.

Rae helped Dana into her coat then grabbed her purse from the couch. When she picked up Dana's keys, including the tiny pink taser dangling like dangerous décor, Dana noticed her sister's attention. "I feel better having it, especially walking out to my car. I'll get you one next time I'm at Frankie's."

"Maybe," Rae offered, but she knew that as long as she shared the town with her ex, she'd keep her defense options open. "Sounds like she's got a proper female safety side hustle going," Rae remarked. "I like it."

She gave her sister one final quick inspection. "Have a good day at school," she joked, giving her a pat on the shoulder.

"Thanks, Mom." Dana winked at her sister and walked out the door. She still had plenty of time before dark. They'd been more careful about walking home alone at night lately but springing for rides took a bite out of their budget. Their best defenses were daylight and crowds, and the night shift offered one but not the other.

Rae checked her watch. She'd wait a half hour before venturing out. The lies had already begun: telling Dana that she gave up a shift to someone who needed the hours more even though she'd begged off work. She needed the day for recon. She walked to her bedroom and pulled the burner from a folded pillowcase in her bottom drawer. She made a pot of coffee and settled in with her laptop and the phone. She'd do a little online research before venturing out to meet her mark. She hated this version of herself, but she also knew that a better version would never emerge unless this one did her job.

She pulled the crumpled paper from her purse and stared at Victor's chicken scratch handwriting, distinctive enough that Dana would certainly recognize it. She typed the man's name into the search bar and found precious little about him until she happened upon his social media. Here he was, showcasing a flashy car with gold bling around his neck, broadcasting his supposed wealth to five thousand followers. She shook her head as she scrolled. She quickly found his favorite bar and restaurant. For someone who made a living stealing other people's property, Trent Frye didn't seem too concerned about keeping his lifestyle a secret. She chuckled at his tagline underneath this handle: *entrepreneur.*

Rae fished around her bag until she pulled the burner from the inside pocket. Victor had sent her a message about Trent's schedule. She just had to wait for his location. Victor was always good at keeping tabs on people.

She just had to steal one little thing. In and out. No problem.

Rae considered working in casinos to be a test of will. She'd been sober just shy of a year, and for the first six months, the Sin City circuit almost broke her. Her sponsor, Emil, warned her that it was unwise to test her resolve in such a way. She considered it a necessary training. If Wiley ever found her, she'd need to be stronger, and this was her way of building up that power. If she could not only be around alcohol each day but also serve it, she'd be commanding enough to deal with him if he ever crossed her path again, which was likely since he still called Vegas home.

Rae navigated to the address Victor had sent. Most people didn't realize how quickly Vegas morphed from a 24-hour light show into a regular town with battered strip malls and suburban neighborhoods. Some fast-food franchises leaned with glittery lights on their signs, but it didn't take much travel to realize that only a sliver of the city proved compelling to tourists. For the locals, it was just another place to live, work, and pass time.

A quick fifteen minutes off the Strip, and Rae found herself pulling into an unremarkable apartment complex that resembled other unremarkable apartment complexes on the same street. Older units, run down, probably good prices if you didn't have standards. It reminded Rae of a hotel that had been converted into apartments. Doors on the outside, metal railing, no frills. While she searched for unit 14210, she drove slowly through the winding parking lot, her eyes checking numbers on each building. When she found it, she pulled into a nearby parking space.

Damn.

Rae hated second floor units, or anything higher level. Breaking into an apartment, or any residential dwelling, was easier without the addition of stairs to navigate in the event of a quick exit. She'd twisted an ankle more than once bolting down a flight or two with contraband in hand.

Victor had sent her the basic information she needed. His yellow Corvette wasn't parked in the lot from where she could see. She stepped out of her gray Camry and walked to a nearby building, not wanting to be seen in Trent's direct space. Rae had the added advantage of average features that, when paired with a baseball cap or an oversized jacket, made her invisible to the male gaze, another necessary tool in her lineup for this job. She kept her sling bag tucked under her arm and walked confidently towards the building. She spotted a young woman walking a small, yappy dog and an older couple getting into a Cadillac. She took note of her surroundings but didn't make eye contact.

The apartment was on the back side of the building, a real gift for anyone involved in escalating from breaking and entering to theft. She walked up the stairs with purpose, glancing over her shoulder for any spectators. None so far. She stood in front of the door. She took note of the worn window screens and the standard key entry.

Rae knocked. Better to make sure now than once she was inside. No answer. She waited a beat. She was sweating now and reminded herself to breathe deeply. She needed to control her adrenaline. She considered turning back on the job but then thought of Dana slinging drinks in those miserable sequined nightmares and refocused her attention. The lock was a standard pin tumbler, so she pulled her tension wrench from her kit, a gift from her dad. It was one of the skills he'd taught her that had proven to be a blessing and a curse for both of them. He'd done some time over stretches of decades, his life a cautionary tale for anyone who keeps taking small steps down the wrong path, doubling down on bad decisions.

She dismissed her father's ghost and focused on the job at hand, working the torque with enough gentle pressure to force the picked pins in place. It felt natural, this movement, like something she could do with her eyes closed. She worked the plug, turning it until she heard a click. She glanced over her shoulder one last time before opening the door.

Rae was greeted with the pungent odor of skunks, and wondered why someone couldn't make weed smell less obnoxious. The stark contrast to Trent's flashy Instagram presence surprised her. The apartment was dreary in a way that old, unloved spaces tended to be: the living room was dark, with old maroon shades drawn to banish sunlight and nosy neighbors.

Rae surveyed the space, which seemed to be more of a storage unit than a living area, with boxes stacked against one wall. She wondered how he managed to get them on the upper floor—what a pain in the ass. A ground floor apartment was more vulnerable, which is why she supposed he'd chosen the second story. A battered leatherette couch and recliner that seemed old enough to remember Carter's presidency anchored the space, but nothing else in the room welcomed guests. The space was littered with boxes, random tools, papers and trash. It was as if a bachelor pad had made a baby with a hoarder's garage.

Rae looked past the boxes into the kitchen, which was a compact galley setup that didn't seem to have any sort of culinary activity outside of hosting takeout boxes. She quickly began opening cabinets. Nothing in any of them.

She made her way to the bedroom, where she discovered a mattress on the floor. What was it with men and their hatred for box springs and linens? No dresser, only a small wooden end table that had seen better days, its surface decorated with white rings and scratches. She moved to the shutter style closet doors and pulled them apart. A stack of blankets covered something, but no clothing. She pulled them away, finding boxes of designer sneakers underneath.

No jewelry.

A quick run through the bathroom yielded nothing.

"This can't be happening," Rae muttered to herself, pulling the mattress off the floor and finding nothing underneath. Nothing inside the pillowcases or the sheets.

She returned to the kitchen. The fridge and freezer were bare save for a few tall boys and random condiments. Who needed mayonnaise and pickles but no proper food? She checked her watch. She was burning time.

She turned to the oven, leaned forward, and pulled the

crusted door open. Her eyes rested on a Dell computer box. She pulled it out, placed it on the stovetop and opened it. Her eyes rested on the diamond and emerald broach, vintage with intricate craftwork. It lay atop a collection of other pieces—watches, necklaces, bracelets, a few small gold bars, a vintage money clip, some chains.

It was only after she closed the box that she noticed a small green light poised above the microwave. Maybe Trent was smarter than Victor had given him credit for. Exposed, Rae did the only thing that made sense.

She took the entire box.

If Trent saw her face, she might as well make the payday worth it.

Rae held the burner phone to hear ear as she left the parking lot.

"You all done?" he asked.

"We've got a problem, Victor." Rae struggled to keep her voice even. She could feel a quiver bubbling up in her throat. "Pretty sure Trent's got some sort of recording setup. I saw it when I was inside."

"Did you find the piece?"

"Yes, but I need to know where to meet you. He knows my face now, Victor."

"Just get back here and we'll figure it out."

Rae hung up the phone and tossed it on the passenger's seat. Her thoughts traveled to Dana and how she would explain what happened. She'd put her sister in danger now because she broke their one rule.

Don't call Victor.

Rae pulled into the parking lot of the EZ Stay hotel and took a deep breath before reaching over for the stolen box of who knows what. She knew the dangers of letting her adrenaline hijack her senses. She tucked the box under her arm and opened the driver's side door. She checked over her shoulder before leaving her car. Nothing suspicious and no one paying her any mind.

She knocked on Victor's door and turned the knob. When she opened it, she found Victor sitting behind his paper strewn desk, smoking a cigarette. His eyes glanced to his left, and Rae realized they weren't alone.

"Long time no see," Wiley said, stepping from behind the vanity wall where he'd been lying in wait. He dangled a gun from his right hand. Rae's mind darted to the possibilities, trying to figure out how to get out of the room. She was trapped with the one person she'd worked so hard to leave.

"I didn't realize you and Victor were close," Rae said.

"We're not," Wiley said. "I mean, not anymore. Your fault, by the way." He signaled to her. "I always thought we could work it out. Especially since you left me something to remember you by." He ran his finger along the white scar line on his forearm. He pointed the gun in her direction, and she flinched from the movement. She knew how much he loved witnessing her fear.

Rae refused to take the bait. "What do you want?"

Rae glanced at Victor, who pretended to be a calm witness in this conversation. Rae knew better. They both understood how unpredictable Wiley could be, benevolent one moment and cruel the next.

"You'd be surprised how much I know about you," Wiley said. He turned to Victor. "Vegas is a small town, and I have ways of keeping tabs on you. When I heard you came back for a job, well, I figured it had to be a good haul to make it worth it." He glanced at the box underneath her arm. "I thought it was the perfect time for a little reunion. We could have a drink and celebrate what you brought for me."

She clutched the box tighter under his gaze. Its contents were supposed to buy her freedom, not fund her cruel ex's lifestyle. "I'm sober, Wiley. Not doing anything with you, including drinking."

"I heard that," he said. "Sounds boring." He took a step closer to her. "And I don't remember you being boring."

Rae flinched but didn't step back. She gripped the box and held his stare. Victor stubbed out his cigarette, as if witnessing two friends having a minor disagreement.

"Let's settle this without any injuries, okay?" He tipped his head towards Wiley's weapon, now dangling at his side. "We can cut you in on the deal once I clear payment." He held his hands up. "Everybody wins, no one gets hurt."

"I think I need someone to get hurt," Wiley said, eyes trained on Rae. "This one's got a debt to pay."

Rae clenched her jaw, her skin flushed with fear. She held the box up. "Here, take it and go."

Wiley's smile couldn't disguise the flush of anger in his eyes. He glanced at Victor. "You're going to go out the door first, then Rae, and then me. I have just the place where we can settle this...problem."

Rae wondered if Wiley could feel the panic building in her body. There were few things she was certain of in the world, but she knew if she got in a car with Wiley, she would never see her sister again.

"Let's go," Wiley said, signaling to Victor with the gun. "No need to make a mess here."

Victor hesitated before standing up from his chair. He reached for his cigarettes and lighter, then tucked them in his back pocket as if leaving for a grocery run. He locked eyes with Rae but said nothing. A hot flame of anger traveled through her; she wanted him to resist, but she also knew it was dangerous to do so. She willed herself to come up with a distraction but all she felt was panic.

Victor moved carefully past Wiley and his weapon and then in front of Rae. He stopped short at the door. "Let's settle this, okay?"

Rae watched a flicker of anger in Wiley's eyes. He shoved Victor back into the closed door. "This is all your fault," he yelled.

Rae's fear disappeared and anger took its place. She pushed into him, using her box of stolen contraband as a weapon, a downward motion to strike the gun out of his hand. A cascade of jewelry spilled onto the floor with Wiley's weapon lost in the tangle. Rae thew her body on the ground, sharp objects pointing into her stomach and chest as she searched for Wiley's gun. Wiley leaned over, arms scooping underneath her body, and turned her over in a single motion. Victor moved towards her aid a moment too late.

A loud pop sliced through the room and Wiley stumbled backwards into Victor's desk. Time stopped for several seconds as Rae took in her surroundings: Wiley groaned as he held his chest, blood turning his t-shirt crimson.

Rae dropped the gun on the ground, still on her knees. "We need to get help," she said, her voice allowing a small shake of fear to return. Victor moved towards her. He reached his arms around her and helped her stand.

"This wasn't supposed to..." Rae said, her trembling hand in his.

"I'll handle it," he said, his voice softer now. "I'll be in touch. Go home to Dana."

Rae looked into Victor's eyes and nodded. She turned her

back to Wiley, who had folded to the floor in a fit of grunts and labored breath.

She pulled the door closed behind her, walked to her car, and wept.

Rae watched as her sister carried two cardboard boxes to her Toyota. Trunk open, she maneuvered them until they fit into the already full space, then closed the latch.

"If you've got anything else, better ship it, sell it, or leave it."

Dana shook her head. "You want to give the place one last look?"

Rae shook her head. "Nope. I don't want to see this apartment or this town ever again."

She unzipped the front pocket of her backpack and placed her hand on a white envelope, just to make sure it was still safe. Victor made good on his promise, giving her enough money to start over and slipping Trent an inside scoop on another job. She knew nothing about Wiley. Neither would utter his name.

Of course, she knew she would never really be free of him. No matter where she traveled, he would be tucked in some tiny corner of her mind.

"Hand me the keys," Dana said, her hand outstretched. "I'll take the first leg."

Rae dropped her keys in Dana's palm and slipped into the passenger's side. She clutched the backpack in her lap as her sister started the engine.

She refused to look behind her but instead turned her face towards the sun. The ghosts would follow her anyway.

ABOUT THE AUTHORS

You can learn more about the authors at their websites.
   https://alexandraburt.com
   https://vpchandler.com/
   https://lauraoles.com/

www.ingramcontent.com/pod-product-compliance
Lightning Source LLC
Chambersburg PA
CBHW050414110726
47899CB00008B/2716